SAN ANSELMO LIBRARY
110 TUNSTEAD AVENUE
SAN ANSELMO, CA 9496

Y0-AAW-249

Purchased with Library Parcel Tax funds.
Thank You San Anselmo Residents!

DISCARDED

AUG 1 7 2016

DATE DUE

Demco

Weather to Fly

CHRISTOPHER LEGRAS

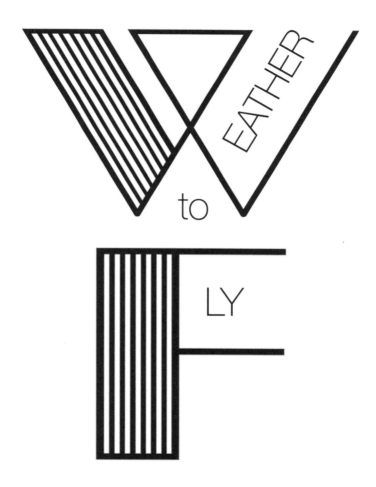

WEATHER to FLY

a novel
in stories

THIS IS A GENUINE VIREO BOOK

A Vireo Book | Rare Bird Books
453 South Spring Street, Suite 302
Los Angeles, CA 90013
rarebirdbooks.com

Copyright © 2016 by Christopher LeGras

FIRST HARDCOVER EDITION

All rights reserved, including the right to reproduce this book or portions thereof in any form whatsoever, including but not limited to print, audio, and electronic. For more information, address: A Vireo Book | Rare Bird Books Subsidiary Rights Department, 453 South Spring Street, Suite 302, Los Angeles, CA 90013.

Set in Minion
Printed in the United States

For the purposes of clarity, the editor and the author have taken style liberties to depict dialog in italics, and with models of planes when they are mentioned in dialog.

10 9 8 7 6 5 4 3 2 1

Publisher's Cataloging-in-Publication data

Names: LeGras, Christopher, author.
Title: Weather to fly : a novel in stories / by Christopher LeGras.
Description: First Hardcover Edition | A Vireo Book | Los Angeles [California] ; New York [New York] : Rare Bird Books, 2016.
Identifiers: ISBN 978-1-942600-18-3.
Subjects: Airplanes—Fiction. | Flight—Fiction. | Family—Fiction. | Short stories, American. | Adventure—Fiction. | BISAC: FICTION / Literary. | GSAFD: Tall tales.
Classification: LCC PS3612.E353 W43 2016 | DCC 813.6—dc23.

To W. Dean LeGras (1937-2006)
7,872 hours

Never trust the teller; trust the tale.
—D. H. Lawrence

One thing you don't do, you don't believe anything anybody tells you about an airplane.
—Chuck Yeager

Itinerary

Pre-Flight

This little volume contains some flying stories. Some of them are true and others are made up. The rest, which is to say most of them, fall somewhere in between. The majority are about airplanes and pilots, but a couple are about birds, and there's one that's mostly about an airport terminal but is also a love story. They're all adventure tales in their own way.

We should mention there are also a couple three in which flying is a metaphor for something else and airplanes only appear in the periphery. These stories are a little different and you'll recognize them by what the great American philosopher Mack called hooptedoodle. They have a little more décor than the others and like old Mack said, they try to sing a song or two, maybe paint a pretty picture. That's just the storyteller opening it up a bit, like a pilot who throws a few barrel rolls and loop-the-loops into a flight. As any aerobat will tell you, even when she's carrying paying customers experiencing the thrill of an open cockpit and inverted flight for the first time, those loop-the-loops and barrel rolls are still mostly hers. We'll readily admit it can be downright selfish on the part of the pilot or the writer, which is maybe why not every passenger likes to loop-the-loop and not every reader likes hooptedoodle. And so out of deference to differences in taste those stories make themselves known pretty quickly so that the reader can take them or leave them as she pleases.

Not that we're suggesting the regular stories are straight-and-level the whole way. There's one about an Air Force fighter jock who acquires a mysterious wingman, another is about a broken heart, and there are a couple about a World War II warbird that may or may not have a soul and a conscience. There are honest-to-goodness war stories, ghost stories, tall tales, and stories that pilots will swear are true even though they aren't in any history books or old news accounts. The true stories have been stretched and embellished by retelling so that they might sound more fabulous than the made-up ones, but don't let that fool you. A man or woman who lives a story only lives a fraction of it, especially if the experience involves subjects like love, life, death, or an emergency landing. That kind of story happens so fast that after it's all over and the man or woman sits down in the tavern years later and tells it he or she usually discovers there's not much to tell at all. Even worse, the part there is to tell is so scrambled it lands on its audience with a thud and hardly merits a glass of beer on the house.

Of course there are exceptions, but in our experience this is a dependable generalization. It's only in the retelling and the re-retelling and so forth that the details emerge like the constellations in a twilight sky and the story gains its fullest expression. Pilots nurture stories like children: each teller contributes his or her experience in the hope that he or she can make it a little better, a little wiser. It's far from a novel metaphor (if you'll pardon the pun) but it explains a great deal about why storytellers, meaning all of us, tell stories. Each retelling adds to a story's development and maturity until one day it mostly stops changing. When it comes to flying stories pilots distinguish instinctively a story that needs guidance from one that's done growing, the subtle difference between *it couldn't have happened like that* and *it didn't happen like that.* By the time you finish with this little volume of flying stories you'll have an idea of how to tell the two kinds of stories apart. If we accomplish that then our time together will have been well spent.

Meanwhile it will help to bear in mind that truth has different connotations at 30,000 feet. Facts are just the beginning, and as often as not they just confuse matters. Think of the stories that follow as primers to a world that's bigger than any of us can imagine.

That about completes our pre-flight.

A final word: don't worry should we encounter headwinds, fog, icy conditions, even enemy fire. The characters and storytellers in this little volume have spent a good part of their lives aloft, and we're in excellent hands indeed…

The Ballad of
Kandy Kim, Part 1

Do not spin this aircraft. If the aircraft does enter a spin it will
return to earth without further attention on the part of the aeronaut.
—Manual issued with the first Curtis-Wright Flyer in 1909

Kandy Kim was a P-38D Lightning twin-engine fighter that rolled off the Lockheed assembly line in Burbank, California on June 7, 1944, not thirty-six hours after the Allies' great and terrible victory on the D-Day beaches in Normandy. When she was towed into the sunlight on the shimmering asphalt tarmac for the first time she was P-38D No. 1138-926-8-42, and in her olive drab paint and US Army Air Corps livery she was identical to the forty-two other P-38Ds that came off the lines that day. We can verify that her construction required sixty-six men and women and that it took 5,700 tooling hours from her first rivet to her final coat of paint, plus another 447 hours at a modification center to ready her for the winter duty to which she had been assigned in Alaska. Were we so inclined we could even ascertain the names of those sixty-six men and women with a telephone or email request to the Air Force archives. However, we know the Lockheed worker who had the distinction of giving Kandy Kim her name. For purposes of understanding Kim the other sixty-five are rather superfluous (that's a good example of a fact that would clutter things up).

His name was Gytis Vygantas, and he was a first generation Lithuanian-American Jew from the city of Klaipėda. His family was among the few who escaped the German occupation that began in 1939, when Gytis was fourteen years old. When the United States entered World War II on December 8, 1941 he was one of the first men in line at the Army recruitment station in Los Angeles, where his family had settled after time in Flushing, New York and Skokie, Illinois. He wanted nothing more than to wear the American uniform and fight the Germans, but unfortunately for Gytis he was born with a left leg that was two inches shorter than his right. He was designated 4-F without so much as a physical. The recruiting officer took one look at his leg, and the clunky shoe with the big sole he wore on his left foot, and simply shook his head.

Gytis was gravely disappointed, but he was not the sort of man to let disappointment hold him back. Having fled certain death in the face of the Nazi war machine as a young teenager, Gytis had perspective on life's travails. If he couldn't fight, then by God he'd do his part some other way. He got a job at the Lockheed plant as a rivet catcher, then a riveter, and a week before D-Day he was promoted to welder. Kandy Kim was the first airframe he touched with his torch.

As we mentioned No. '8-42 rolled off the assembly line less than two days after D-Day. More importantly for our story, it was also less than a week after Gytis became a father for the first time. He and his wife named their baby girl after her mother's mother Kornelija, a nurse in World War I who died in August 1918 during the darkest days of the Battle of the Somme. Before '8-42 was towed out to the tarmac, Gytis penned an oil-stained note in broken English signed with a Mishnah and a Star of David and taped it to the pilot's seat. The note asked that '8-42 be named in his daughter's honor.

That very afternoon '8-42's first pilot discovered the note. Nora Hall was a thirty-one-year-old Women Airforce Service Pilot, better known as a WASP, from Tacoma, Washington. She'd been ferrying new fighters throughout the United States and Europe since July of '43. A ranch girl originally from the Wyoming plains, Nora started driving her daddy's tractor when she was twelve, had gotten her driver license at fifteen, her pilot's license at seventeen, and her teaching certificate at twenty-one. She had been a high school health teacher and a graduate student at the University of Washington until she learned the government had formed the WASP Corps. She was Washington state's first volunteer.

Nora could only make out about half of Gytis's message but she got the gist. She felt that Kornelija was a bit exotic for the US Army Air Corps so she shortened it to Kim. In the flight manifest transmitted via cable to the 344th Fight Squadron Headquarters at Elmendorf Field in Anchorage, the Notes column next to '8-42's entry said, *Kandy Kim, named for Kornelija Vygantas, Los Angeles, CA.* Nora put Gytis's note in the little compartment in Kim's cockpit where her manual, logbook, and service record were kept. It remains there to this day.

As you might have guessed, Kandy Kim proved to be anything but just another P-38D. She quickly became famous throughout the Army Air Corps, for Kim sometimes flew where she pleased and how she saw fit, unconcerned with what her pilot may have had in mind or her mission parameters. The men (and women) who flew her came to believe she was possessed by a mischievous spirit. Her reputation circulated and grew, and every mission added a new facet, a new wrinkle to the legend. Kandy Kim's puckish exploits also gave rise to stories about other airplanes, or maybe gave other pilots the courage to tell their tales. The marines talked about a Chance Vought F4U-1 Corsair carrier-based fighter that was badly damaged by Japanese anti-aircraft fire over Guadalcanal but managed to fly her critically wounded, unconscious pilot back to the USS *Saratoga* and land herself in the midst of a squall. The Brits claimed an Avro Lancaster four-engine heavy bomber started up all by itself one morning before dawn and took off from Stendstall Field in Essex. Air Command scrambled four Supermarine Spitfires to intercept her, but the pilots watched in disbelief as the bomber flew itself into the path of a V-2 rocket that otherwise would have landed in central London and killed thousands.

In contrast to the men and women who serve in them, militaries cannot abide anything resembling superstition, least of all in wartime. For every story about airplanes performing miracles to save their crews or aid their countries' fight, military leadership and government bureaucrats offered the sorts of explanations that seemed logical to the sorts of people who populate military leadership and government bureaucracies. The Marine Commandant reported the Corsair involved in the *Saratoga* incident had not flown itself at all, but that her pilot had stayed conscious long enough to make it home. His injuries and blood loss simply caused a short-term memory failure. The Commandant's conclusion was dutifully reported in *Stars and Stripes* and the censor cut the paragraph in which the pilot, Lt. J. G. Maxwell Ross, stated that he remembered the exact moment he lost consciousness some 200 nautical miles from the carrier and still over enemy territory. Likewise, the British government announced the Lancaster, dubbed London's Saviour, was in fact piloted by a German double agent who knew the rocket's launch coordinates and target vectors but was unsuccessful in persuading Air Command to plan an intercept (the Brits apparently concluding, in a foretaste of the postwar world, that the public would find mortal bureaucratic ineptitude and suicide more palatable than divine intervention or the supernatural).

So it was with Kandy Kim. Her exploits were easier to conceal from the official news outlets than the others because she was based on a remote Alaskan island and because she never saw combat. And so when one day Kim proved too mischievous for her own good and her left supercharger blew at the apex of a too-aggressive Immelman on a training flight, it didn't even register. Besides, the Army Air Corps was preparing for the atomic bomb drops on Hiroshima and Nagasaki and couldn't be bothered to investigate a phantom P-38 in the frozen north.

Kandy Kim crash-landed on a glacier, and it preserved her for the better part of a century (not to worry, her stupefied pilot was rescued within a couple hours). It's true, some glaciers have a weakness for airplanes, and it was Kandy Kim's good fortune that she found one of them. Then again, planes like her always seem to land in luck.

That might have been the end of the story, but Kandy Kim had other ideas. From time to time over the years bush pilots and military pilots reported observing what appeared to be a downed twin-engine airplane in a crevasse on the Hubbard Glacier near Yakutat. Once she even showed up on an Air Force satellite image. She showed herself just often enough to become a sort of talisman among Alaska fliers and to keep her legend alive in the Air Force.

Finally, Kandy Kim's resting place was revealed to two members of a clan of nomadic bards one night two Julys ago at the King Salmon Saloon in Kodiak. A seventy-seven-year old bush pilot called Derringer Bill, who claimed to have apprehended his own demise at the controls of a Cessna 180 float over the Alagnak River, spent what he believed was his last night on Earth drinking bourbon and unburdening his soul of its secrets.

The biggest secret of all, the one that cost the fellows the better part of a bottle of Wild Turkey to loosen from his lips, was that he was the only man alive who knew Kandy Kim's resting place. He was old enough to have flown in the war but, like many Alaskans, his own story began later in 1968 when he moved to the last frontier.

Moreover, whether or not he was Kandy Kim's pilot on that final flight was neither here nor there. In the dark saloon with walls adorned with taxidermied fish and faded framed pictures of bush pilots, the fellows asked him the obvious, why he'd never recovered her for himself.

He replied, *Let's just say there's a good reason she ended up in that glacier.* As he skimmed the edge of unconsciousness and talked to pilots who'd been gone for many years, the fellows took notes in shorthand:

You wanna take off with full tanks from the old field at Fort Glenn. That's on the north side of Umnak Island. Yeah, it's important you start way the Hell out there. Now quit interruptin'. When you hit a thousand on your climb out, turn east-north-east and follow the panhandle until you hit Seward. Don't bother with the 'lectric compass and fer Chrissake stay north of Kodiak Island. There are bad things to the south.

When you make the bay keep your course 'til you overfly an inlet what looks like a bikini girl doin' a swan dive. Her left leg points to the Sustina River. Glacier's at the headwater, beyond Talkeetna. Kim's next to a red splotch on a big crevasse on the south face, shaped like a spawning humpie. But I gotta warn you, you'll only see her if she wants you to. It's like the old song says, she's funny that way.

Such is the way bush pilots see the world and God love 'em for it. As far as the fellows have been able to determine, no 180s went down in Alaska that summer. In fact, no one in Kodiak, no one anywhere, could recall a pilot named Derringer Bill. Something told the fellows that didn't matter quite as much as the story he'd told and the waypoints he revealed.

And damned if he wasn't right.

The fellows followed his instructions to the letter, three of them in a Beech Bonanza V-tail starting off from the abandoned ghost of an airfield at the end of the Aleutian Chain. They saw Kim, all right. Not only that, the fellows called the clan together and four dozen men and women from a dozen countries worked six weeks to rescue her from the ice. Two of the oldest and oddest fellows, who claimed lineage from Peter the Great and disappeared for seven weeks every winter to visit their homeland in Minsk, arranged for Kandy Kim to be carried home aboard a converted A-90 Orlyonok amphibious transport. Being every bit Kim's equals in tomfoolery they painted the massive craft like Further from *The Electric Kool-Aid Acid Test.*

Between the aircraft identification, its altitude (an Orlyonok is a sort of half-plane, half-hovercraft that flies in ground effect precisely five feet above the water and leaves quite a rooster tail in its wake) and its pilots' inexplicable accents, it took the two fellows at the Orlyonok's controls several tries to explain themselves to air traffic control once they were out of the Alaska and British Columbia wilds and into the orderly airspace of the continental United States. It also took a goodly amount of patience, a quality for which this particular clan, and the particular fellows at the Orlyonok's controls, are not noted. The Air National Guard scrambled three different pairs of interceptors between Seattle and Los Angeles to keep an eye on them. Then again, maybe the pilots just wanted to record *Orlyonok intercept* in their logbooks. Those sorts of things matter to fighter pilots.

At last Kandy Kim arrived in California at Van Nuys Airport, not twenty miles from where she emerged from the Lockheed plant in '44. A convoluted and admittedly archaic contractual arrangement precludes us from disclosing her owner (to the extent a gal like Kim can be owned in any sense of the word). Rest assured she's in good hands.

She did require a bit of TLC, of course, before she was airworthy again. That many years in deep freeze takes a toll even on a plane as rugged as Kim. The clan's greatest smithy, specially flown in aboard an equally outrageous craft from his homeland where the sun that time of year shined nineteen hours a day and twice on Thursdays, miraculously saved everything but her left wingtip. With Kim's permission, so he claimed, he repurposed it into a desk before forging a new one and completing her refurbishment.

The desk circulated within and among the clan for a while, each woman and man getting a few good stories out of it before passing it along. The stories were of such quality and proved so popular that the fellows, who until meeting Kandy Kim had supported themselves by ghostwriting famous authors through writer's block (you'd be amazed who's used them over the years), were able to buy three more airplanes, a hot air balloon, and their first small dirigible (which, for reasons known only to themselves, they named the Leap Year Blimp).

Finally, it came time to part with the desk. The clan had a regular stall at the East Highlands Farmers' Market in Los Angeles and one day last fall a group of wayward writers saw the desk and inquired after it. After a bit of haggling that everyone recognized as a formality the fellows tending the stall sold the desk for a sum that would hardly have purchased a box of heirloom tomatoes.

These days you might spot it at a fiction reading in East LA, a poetry slam in the San Gabriel Mountains, or an art installation in the Mojave Desert. It lifts off every now and again, reminding us (and occasionally an incredulous visitor) what's really important in our all-too-brief lives.

As for Kandy Kim herself, there will be much more to tell. For now, the fellows are putting her through her paces and helping her get used to a world of turbojets, GPS, fly-by-wire, and Pulse-Doppler radar.

Of course, they tell stories all the while.

Riding the 'Cane

Sometimes things are bigger than you, and the best you can hope for is to keep your wings level and have patience and a little luck.
—*Warren L. "Wally" Simpson, World War II bomber pilot*

J asper Wolfskill was in a pickle. In itself this wasn't unusual. After all, a crow learns pretty quickly about tight spots. One of his pop's favorite stories was about the time when he was fifteen moons old and found himself trapped in the back of a garbage truck. Asked how he came to find himself in such a predicament, Pop would puff out his chest and say, *Biggest darned piece of chicken fried steak I ever laid eyes on, that's how*. In addition to being a raconteur, Jasper's pop was something of a gourmand.

He'd flown down to a green city dumpster a couple of blocks from the Santa Monica shoreline and tucked right into that greasy, salty, crusty, just-spoiled-enough-to-make-a-crow's-beak-water chunk of meat when something clonked him on the noggin and everything went black as his feathers. He came to bouncing in the back of what he surmised via olfaction was a garbage truck. He gave a quick, silent thanks to the garbage men for not pushing the red button on the side of the truck that caused the whole back end to collapse on itself and crush the trash—along with any errant scavengers—to make room for more trash. It was crow's luck and Maynard Wolfskill knew better than to push it. He needed out, and now.

I tell you, he'd say, his deep blue eyes glinting with the playfulness Jasper loved in his old bird, *I was in a tight spot and I didn't have long before it got a lot tighter, know what I mean?* At which point the other crows on the telephone line or in the palm tree would caw and twitter in the camaraderie to which Jasper had aspired even before his first moonday. Pop's audience, who had heard the story at least a hundred times, would (if you'll forgive the expression) egg him on. *What'd you do, Maynard? How'd you get outta there, old crow?*

His father would grow somber, almost philosophical. If he had a twig handy (oh, how Pop loved his twigs) he'd use it to scratch at a mite in his chest feathers or preen a wing as if he'd lost his train of thought. Pop was a master suspense builder when he told stories, a skill that earned him the nickname The Bard. The moniker actually was dispensed by an irate cormorant at Point Dume who'd had quite enough of Maynard's crow stories, but Pop owned it right away and turned the tables as only a crow can.

After a few moments of scratching, preening, or just gazing toward the sage green Santa Monica Mountains, he'd say, *Instinct.*

Crows have the best instincts of any bird species in the world except Northern Wheateaters. But those guys are just freaks of nature.

There'd be the requisite, *Whaddya mean, Maynard? Tell us, Maynard! How'd you get outta there, Maynard? Come on, tell us!*

His father would answer, *A crow never panics. You can put us in any situation you can think of. The worse things seem, the calmer we become. Remember Old Bill?*

Asking a crow if he'd heard of Old Bill was like asking a pigeon if she'd heard of a bird named Cher Ami or inquiring a human being about a fellow called Lindbergh. Old Bill saved the crows of New Orleans from Hurricane Katrina. As the storm gathered strength on that fateful August afternoon, instead of panicking like the other birds, the crows had flocked to their usual meeting spot in the willows near the Palace Café on Canal Street. They weren't particularly frightened but they were at something of a loss as to what to do. No one had ever seen a storm like this one. Crows being crows, everyone had an idea and no one could agree. They cawed like mad, each bird straining to raise his or her voice over the others' and the growing menace in the Gulf.

Old Bill, who at that point was a middle-aged nester named William Gadfly known mostly for his crossed beak, the result of an unfortunate encounter with a tourist fanboat on Bayou Chevee, had an idea. The storm was too big to fly around and everyone knew that trying to fly against a hurricane was suicide. Bill suggested they fly *with* it. The idea was too much even for crows, and they cawed something fierce.

Calm as could be, Bill (who was more than forty moons old) lifted off and corkscrewed high into the air. As they watched, the crows' disbelief turned to amazement, and then euphoria. Riding the pressure at the edge of the hurricane Bill streaked through the sky like a black peregrine falcon. He tumbled and cartwheeled, sometimes seeming to lose control only to roll back to level flight. A few brave souls joined him, then a few more, and as the first raindrops fell on the doomed city 10,000 crows rode the pressure and flew to safety. Ever since, *riding the 'cane* was the highest form of crow praise for a well-executed aerial maneuver, and calling someone Old Bill was the greatest compliment in crowdom.

Pop would continue. *I asked myself what Old Bill would do. I sure as shingles wasn't going to peck my way through a steel-hulled garbage truck, and if I'd tried to fly I'd likely have broken a wing or cracked my head. It was black as a feather. Still, the longer I was in there the calmer I felt. You know how it is. Finally I realized the truck was built by human beings, and human beings are ground animals. The answer was probably as close to the ground as you could get. I pecked through the garbage (how it pained me to leave that magnificent chicken fried steak behind!) until I got to the bottom. I felt along the edge and sure enough I found a switch. A tap of my beak and the big machine went to work. The giant hatch started to open and as soon as I saw daylight I was out of there like a gerfalcon! The mess on Ocean Street fed the local crows for a week even after the humans cleaned up what they could.*

Of course everyone knew that last part best of all. The Garbage Deluge was one of the great feasts in Southern California crow lore.

In his current predicament Jasper was beginning to worry that he was no Maynard Wolfskill, much less an Old Bill. He didn't feel calm. In fact, it was taking a goodly amount of mental and emotional energy not to break into a full-blown, very un-crowlike panic.

He was learning to fly. More precisely, he was trying to figure out how to get off the ground. Instincts or no instincts, *flying* was about as far from his mind as chicken fried steak. He would have been content just to get airborne, thrilled with a little awkward gliding.

The moment had been coming for a moon. It started with Mama making a peculiar reference after dinner one night to *Getting you kids out into the big colors.* Then Pop started talking to Jasper and his brothers and sisters about *the great wild mystery.* Words like *big* and *wild* and *mystery* made the quills on the back of Jasper's neck stand up. He was happy at home, and the more Mama and Pop talked the more he found himself half-burrowing his way to the very back of the nest, hiding under his brothers' and sisters' downy feathers.

As if they sensed his anxiety Mama and Pop let him go last. Their good intentions only made him feel worse. All week he'd watched in sick horror as one by one Mama nudged his sisters and brothers to the edge of the nest and heaved them over. Jasper nearly regurgitated his regurgitated breakfast every time he heard another sibling *caaaaawwww*ing his or her way toward the ground. The first one to go was his big sister, Grace. He was convinced she was dead.

Far from it. Grace, like all four of his siblings, miraculously reappeared under her own power a few minutes after her harrowing departure. All of them changed in that tiny window of time. Their eyes glinted more brightly than he'd ever seen, like a light switched on in a human window. They held themselves with their chests puffed out like Pop. Even his little sister Aubrey, who cracked her shell two whole days after Jasper, stood on the edge of the nest glowing like an angel. She'd said, *You can do it, Jasp, I know you can!* He was sure he'd seen doubt in her eyes.

This morning the inevitable had arrived. It wasn't so much plummeting from the top of the palm tree toward the grass. He'd been too terrified to be terrified during the fall. Truthfully, even though it was less than five minutes ago he hadn't the foggiest idea how he'd avoided certain death. He didn't remember spreading his wings, and he knew for a fact he hadn't flown anywhere because he was in a clump of shrubs and yucca not ten wingspans from the base of the palm tree. He was clinging to a dead yucca branch and trying not to look down at the waves crashing on the rocks a hundred feet below.

Finally persuaded that he was not, in fact, dead, he began to assess just how dire his situation was.

As it happened, *dire* didn't begin to cover it. He forced himself to half-look over his shoulder at the cliff and the rocks and the waves and spray. His heart did a somersault and he felt breakfast coming up for what seemed like the tenth time that morning. Since he couldn't fly off, his Plan B (a crow always has a Plan B, and C, and D) was to side-walk his way along the branch to the ground. But when he tried to take even a half step, the branch gave way and he nearly tumbled off. So he clung there, trying to move as little as possible and praying that the branch didn't snap off altogether. The wind picked up and shook the whole plant. Jasper wanted to cry.

Mama was cawing something at him from the nest (easy for her to caw from all the way up there where it was warm and safe and there wasn't a cliff and rocks and ocean below her). Pop flew down from an adjoining palm and hovered a few feet above him. He cawed, *Jasper, Jasper, Jasper!* (Crows tend to repeat themselves when they're excited.) *What are you doing, boy? Spread your wings! Trust your instincts! Come on, son, let's go! Let's go, let's go, let's go!*

It wasn't exactly a heartfelt pep caw. Jasper could hear the frustration, maybe even disappointment, in his father's voice. It made him feel worse. If even Pop, the crow who believed anything was possible, didn't have faith in him, what did that say about his chances of getting out of this fix alive?

He cawed back, humiliated at how terrified he knew he sounded, *I can't! Look at this branch! It'll snap off if I even take a deep breath! Help, help, help!*

His father didn't answer but circled twice and then flew back up to his observation post. *Great*, thought Jasper, his heart sinking further, *they're gonna sit up there and watch me die*. Or worse, watch me make a fool of myself and *then* die. Instincts, my tail feathers. I don't need instincts, I need the nest and a good meal. I need a nap.

At the thought of sleep and the nest he relaxed, kind of. He realized he was more exhausted than he'd ever been in his entire life. His terror ebbed into the fatigue and he saw a warm yellow light in his mind's eye. That was it, he would just take a little nap here on the branch. He would take a nap and when he woke up maybe Pop would have carried him up to the nest and put a little lint over him like he liked. He knew some parents gave their kids a few chances to learn to fly. As Jasper drifted toward the yellow light he was certain of it. Pop would rescue him.

Pop was cawing at him again, more urgently, but Jasper didn't hear what his father was saying. Mama joined in and she sounded even more upset. But Jasper was slipping closer to that warm yellow light, which he realized looked like the nest. Oh, the nest! Maybe his sisters and brothers would come back. He'd rest a day or two, tucked in the warm down of his siblings. When he was ready they'd help teach him to fly. There'd be no shove out of the nest, no hurtling earthward, no clinging to a yucca branch in gusty wind over a cliff of death. He loved his brothers and sisters, and they loved him and would care for him. Jasper felt warmer and warmer even as his parents cawed like mad and the wind blew harder.

For the rest of their moons, Maynard and Martha Wolfskill swore they didn't see the cat until the last second. It was black and it had spent the minutes Jasper clung to the branch slinking through the undergrowth. Slowly, with feline patience, she moved within striking distance at the precise moment when Jasper succumbed to his trance.

Mama saw the cat an instant too late. She dove out of the tree as the beast leaped from the bush and took a vicious swipe at her son. She cawed louder than she'd ever cawed, and dove straight for the black back caring nothing for her own safety. Her instinct to protect her son took over her mind and her body. She wanted blood. An instant later Maynard was right behind her.

Jasper never saw the cat. He didn't hear Mama and Pop screaming at it like screech owls. The cat's razor-sharp claws sliced the air and missed his tail feathers by a quill's width. They sliced his branch and sent him plummeting down the cliff to the rocks and the surf.

He never saw the cat, but he would remember every nanosecond of the fall the rest of his life. At first it felt unreal, and he didn't actually believe that he was watching the yucca tree and the ledge streaking away from him or that the branch to which he'd clung was suddenly level with his head. He felt like he was tumbling very, very slowly, until he was falling beak first. He was perplexed for another endless moment. The ocean was racing toward him at mortal speed. That wasn't right, was it? He caught a whiff of sage in his nostril, and it tickled his eyes. He thought, *I didn't know death smelled like sage.*

As the rocks rushed toward him, he felt something. At first it was just the sense of a sensation. Between him and the cliffs and rocks was a sort of cushion of air. It felt almost like the bottom of the nest, and at the thought of the nest he flashed to a memory of wrestling with his brothers and sisters, falling over and over in the downy bed. Then he felt it under his belly for sure, a slight difference in pressure caused by him moving through it and by the proximity of the rocks that threatened to crush his fragile body. Mama would later explain something called *ground effect.*

He saw the warm yellow light again. Only now the color was deeper, nearly gold, and it wasn't in his mind but all around him in the air. It enveloped him and hugged him and he felt safe. Safer than in his egg, safer than in the nest, safer even than in Mama's wings. As the rocks rushed toward him he reached for the golden light to see what it felt like and what it was made of. He stretched out his wings as far as he could as if he was reaching for a great and perhaps final secret in the instant before his demise.

And he was flying. The sea rocks and sea foam and water rushed at him but the light was above it and around it. He reached for the light again and executed a perfect snap roll around the closest rock, missing it by a barb. Now the golden light lay above the surface of the water like mist and he reached for it there. His snap roll resolved into straight-and-level flight a few feet above the whitecaps.

From somewhere behind him he heard Pop cawing like a bird possessed. Jasper realized he was losing altitude. Pop cawed again and Jasper forced himself to take his eyes off the transfixing light and look over his shoulder. Above him the light was bands of gold and pale purple, and his father was racing toward him flapping almost as fast as a hummingbird.

Jasper looked back at the ocean surface. The light above it had changed into the same sort of gold and purple, the colors woven like a palm frond. He tried to touch a purple band but missed it. He tried and missed again. He kept trying and kept missing, and a funny thing happened. He was flapping his wings. He was no longer losing altitude and heading for the water. He was climbing.

When he'd flapped a few more times, the purple faded and then almost vanished and he was once more bathed in gold. He stopped flapping as an updraft from the cliff caught his wings and his belly. He was maybe 200 feet above the water now, gliding in a slow figure eight as the current ebbed and flowed.

Pop and Mama caught up with him. Pop was as pale as a mourning dove and Mama's eyes were as wide as a puffin's.

Mama reached him first. *Jasper, Jasper, Jasper, Jasper! Son, we thought we'd lost you! Lost you, lost you, lost you!*

Jasper had already forgotten the terror of clinging to the yucca branch. He'd forgotten the nauseating fall from the nest and Mama nudging him out. In fact, he was forgetting more with each flap. He reached for a pale purple band and looped over Mama. *Aw, Mama. Don't make a big deal. It was just a dive. You guys do it all the time.*

Pop leveled off next to them. His color had returned and there was a huge grin in his blue eyes. He didn't say anything at first, but just looked at his son. Then he started laughing. As he laughed the gold and purple around him gave way to a deep orange light and Pop was hovering. *Caaaaw, caw, caw, caw, caw! Didja see that, Martha! First time Jasp flies and he rides the 'cane! A danged snap roll against a cliff! Takes most crows moons to learn that kind of maneuver! Caw, caw, caw, caw, caw! Jasper, boy, you're a natural! Our boy's a real Old Bill!*

Mama started laughing too as Pop flipped onto his back in midair and grabbed his belly with his wings, cackling uncontrollably. He dropped down and away from them, then caught himself and climbed back up, still choking back giggles.

Jasper saw tears of laughter in his parents' eyes. The light filled the sky with more colors than he thought possible. There were hundreds of birds in it, climbing, diving, cartwheeling, gliding. It was the most beautiful thing he had ever seen. It was where he belonged. The three of them made a gentle turn toward land and glided home.

Sea-Tac

*And it is of the highest importance that this common meeting-place should
be reached easily, almost instinctively, in the dark, with one's eyes shut.*
—Virginia Woolf

After the accident and settlement it's decided
Alfred should live at home for a while. The
doctors and specialists and therapists all agree
it's the best way for him to ease back into the
real world. That's how they always say it: *Alfred
needs to ease back into the real world after his accident. He's just
fortunate the settlement provides for his care and rehabilitation.*
Alfred himself has no sense of having left the real world in the
first place, but all the doctors and specialists and therapists concur
and so at the age of thirty-five he finds himself parked in his old
bedroom at his parents' house near Sea-Tac Airport.

The transition is hard at first. Before the accident and
settlement he had a great big house in Seattle, on Queen Anne Hill.

He can't remember for sure how long he lived there and he can't remember what he did to afford it, but he remembers the big living room and the bedroom with the oak beam ceiling and windows that looked over Lake Union. He has a particularly vivid memory of standing on the back lawn watching the Blue Angels perform at Sea Fair, especially the part when one of the gleaming blue F/A-18 fighters with the bright yellow US NAVY emblazoned on its wings screamed 300 feet over the house with its afterburners blazing. He remembers that, and there's a girl in the memory but for the life of him he can't remember who she was. His parents don't seem to remember, either.

It's strange living at home like a kid, but at least his old bedroom isn't so bad. His parents left up some of his posters from way back, the one from an Aerosmith concert when he was in high school, and the ones of airplanes. It's on the second floor and he can look out of his window and see the jets taking off and landing a half mile away at Sea-Tac. Their neighborhood of Normandy Park is nestled on a small hill west of the airport. From one window in his room he can see the gymnasium and football field at his old middle school and from the other he can see almost the whole airport over a grove of evergreens. He can see all three runways and the tall cement control tower and the terminals in which he knows there are people on their way to every corner of the world. Most of all he can see the airplanes.

When family and friends call on the telephone to check on him he always tells them what airlines are taking off and landing.

Even though he's thirty-five and living at home with his parents in his old room, no one makes fun of him. When he walks into town everyone is kind and polite. At the coffee shop he gets free donuts and the kids who work at the pizza joint always give him two free slices of pepperoni. People go out of their way to help him. He wonders if they were like this before.

Each night at dinner his mother says, *We're so glad you're home, Alfred.*

His father says, *Yes, compared to the alternatives, we're very glad indeed.*

These exchanges confuse Alfred, who doesn't remember his parents ever being glad about much of anything, much less something he did. Still, he's happy they're happy. Better late than never, as the saying goes.

After a while Alfred gets restless. It's been six months and the doctors and specialists and therapists still agree he still hasn't eased back into the real world. While they have his best interests in mind the practical effect of all their care is that they're driving him nuts. He is a thirty-five year old man, after all, and despite the accident and settlement he still has a lot of living to do.

He decides to get a job.

The decision presents an immediate conundrum: he isn't allowed to drive a car and public transportation is out of the question. That leaves the mall (yech!) the gas station (yawn) or the airport (yay!).

The doctors and specialists and therapists aren't happy with the idea but if there's one thing about Alfred, once he gets a notion in his head, as his father says, you can't blast it out with dynamite. Besides, his parents tell them their son used to fly airplanes himself.

Alfred laughs inside. He's never even been on a plane much less flown one. Still, it's nice they're on his side these days.

His mother says, *We should let him do at least one thing he loves.*

So one Monday morning he goes to the airport. It's a long walk, more than an hour. It doesn't matter, because the whole time Alfred's eyes are on the sky, watching airliners landing and taking off. Normally that distance is out of bounds but his father says, *Damned if he doesn't remember the way.*

His first trip is a bit of a fiasco. His mother walks with him to the terminal and watches him walk into the huge building. He turns and waves at her like he's going on a trip. He passes the baggage carousels and the car rental desks with long lines of people, the Information Desk and the security desk, the big wall of TV screens with the Arrivals and Departures. He takes the escalator upstairs and wanders to the Alaska Airlines gates.

Which is when all hell breaks loose.

Suddenly he's on the floor and people are shouting at him.

How did you get through security?!

Where's your boarding pass?!

How did you get through security?!

Have you had contact with any known terror groups in the last eighteen months?!

How did you get through security?!

It turns out his getting through security is a really big deal. They take him to a small dark room where a man and a woman in dark suits ask him more questions while two security officers stand by the door. The questions and the noise and the excitement confuse him. He just walked into the terminal like a normal person. Good grief, is the world going crazy? He says he's looking for a job but they don't believe him.

They keep him in the small room until his parents arrive and after an hour of answering questions themselves are allowed to take him home.

At dinner his mother says, *We're so glad you're home safe, Alfred. I think this was too big a step.*

And his father says, *Yes, especially considering the alternatives you could have faced today. But we're very glad indeed.*

The next day one of the therapists comes to the house and says gravely, *You see, this is why Alfred has to ease back into the real world slowly. Much more slowly.*

After that it gets trickier for him to go to the airport. He's allowed to go out again, but he just goes to the park down the street and sits on a bench under a big willow tree and watches the ducks and geese in the pond and the kids playing on the slides and swings and the people jogging, skating, and biking past. He meets a few people and it's perfectly pleasant but it's no Sea-Tac. His mother drives by every couple of hours to check on him. Finally after two weeks his mother and father are convinced he's found a place to go where he won't get into trouble. His mother stops driving by, and a few days later Alfred starts going back to the airport. He doesn't like lying to his parents but he needs a job. He'll go bonkers if he can't get one soon.

The second time he visits the airport he's more careful. He knows his mistake was not taking stock of the situation before barging in. Any old fool knows better than to do that. He chalks it up to the accident and settlement and resolves not to make the same mistake twice. He walks past the baggage carousels and the rental car desks with their long lines and rides the escalator up to the departure floor. This time instead of going into the terminal he finds a place to sit.

He sits in a seat across from the Alaska Airlines counters for an hour and then gets thirsty. He walks to an airport shop to buy a Coca-Cola. The girl behind the counter is very nice and doesn't charge him for the can of soda. She talks to him and he tells her he's going to apply for a job. She seems very happy to hear that. He feels much better about this visit.

A few minutes after he returns to his seat he sees another girl. He nearly drops his can of Coca-Cola. She's the most beautiful girl he's ever seen. She has long red hair and a round face and skin that makes him think of the pink roses in the garden at home. She's wearing a blue sundress with white polka dots. As she passes he sees that her face is freckled and she has bright blue eyes.

Something else strikes him, and it's the reason he doesn't talk to her. There's a look on her face, something at the corners of her lips and in the blue of her eyes. She's like one of those Seattle days when you can't tell if the sun is breaking through the clouds or the clouds are racing across the face of the sun. It throws him off, just enough to keep his butt planted in the seat when she walks by less that five feet from him and gets on the escalator to the ground floor. As she passes he smells vanilla, like the smell of the kitchen when his mother makes her famous chocolate chip cookies.

He doesn't see her again for two weeks. But what a time! He becomes a full-time airport employee. His job is to watch the terminal. He gets lunch each day at the Red Robin and they never charge him because he's an airport employee. He takes his lunch break when there's a lull in activity and the wait staff and bar staff and managers talk with him. He never pays for his Coca-Cola breaks at the shop, either. He does the job for the love of the airport and goes home with a few dollars in his pocket every day. He's very proud but he can't tell his parents about the money he's earning because they'd know he's going back to the airport. He keeps the money in a shoebox under his bed. It feels a little adolescent but it will do for now.

The next time he sees her she's wearing a pale yellow dress with blue butterflies on it. It's about the most beautiful dress he's ever seen. Her hair is tied in a ponytail and she's carrying a red purse and pulling a black carry-on.

This time he stands up and introduces himself. She looks at him and smiles but doesn't say anything. He asks if there's anything he can do for her here at the airport, and she smiles but still doesn't answer. Finally he goes for the simple approach and asks her how her day is going. This time her smile fades a little bit and she shrugs.

Alfred is confused. He knows enough about girls to know that if she didn't want to talk to him she wouldn't have stopped, much less smiled at him.

She puts her hands over her ears and shakes her head, then one hand over her mouth and shakes her head again.

He still doesn't understand. She takes a small notepad out of her red purse. She writes something then tears off the page and hands it to him. The note says: *Hi, my name is Mandy. I'm deaf. It's nice to meet you. What's your name?*

Alfred is momentarily seized with panic. He can read just fine but writing is one of the things the doctors and specialists and therapists have said may or may not come back after the accident and settlement.

Mandy seems to sense his discomfort and gives him another note: *It's okay, I can read lips.*

They talk that way for a few minutes and then Mandy gives Alfred a note that says: *It's been lovely talking with you, Alfred. My sister is waiting at the curb, I should go. She worries too much.* She's drawn a little face with crossed eyes and its tongue sticking out. He still has the note. He still has all of them.

Alfred tells her he hopes he'll see her again. She smiles more widely than ever and nods her head. Then she is gone.

Alfred realizes now he has a new duty at his job. It's a promotion, really. His job is to make sure Mandy is all right whenever she comes through the airport. She's told him she travels twice a month to an ear specialist in Los Angeles, always at the same time and always with Alaska Airlines.

Sure enough, two weeks later he sees her in the terminal. It's raining and her sister is stuck in traffic so they have more time to talk. They sit in the terminal while people hurry this way and that. She says the doctors in Los Angeles say they'll be able to restore at least part of her hearing. It's the first time she's told him she wasn't born deaf. It makes him feel closer to her, because he wasn't born the way he is now either. He doesn't tell her that, though. She's so happy about her doctors' news he mostly listens to her and watches her beautiful smile. Then her phone buzzes and she has to go meet her sister.

The next time they meet they go to lunch at the Red Robin. Mandy has told her sister to pick her up two hours later than usual so they can have a proper, unrushed conversation. The sun is shining and they can see Mt. Rainier out the window. The forest around the airport is so green the trees look like they're made out of stained glass. The airplanes gleam as they taxi, takeoff, and land. Mandy and Alfred talk and talk and talk. Sometimes Mandy speaks but she's ashamed of how she knows her voice sounds so mostly she writes even though Alfred tells her she has a beautiful voice, which she does. They discover they have a lot in common. Alfred tells her about the accident and settlement (it's a short story because the details are so hazy). Mandy tells Alfred she lost her hearing seven years ago because of a rare degenerative condition. She says the doctors are doing amazing things and she knows she'll get her ears back. She says it that way and Alfred laughs with her. Then the check comes and Mandy goes to meet her sister.

The fourth time they meet Mandy brings Alfred a present. It's a box of sign language flash cards. At lunch at the Red Robin Alfred told her his parents say he's always been good with languages (what he doesn't remember is that before the accident and settlement he not only flew airplanes but he was a Ph.D. candidate in linguistics at the University of Washington and spoke five languages including Latin).

Sure enough, when he takes the cards home he discovers he can memorize them almost immediately. Alfred is ecstatic.

Better still the mental exercise starts to wake up other parts of his brain, and he begins remembering snippets of other languages. One night at dinner, instead of saying *Please pass the scalloped* potatoes, Mom, he says, *Aio, mater, quantitas magna frumentorum est*. Which actually means, *Why, mother, that is a very large amount of corn*. Still, when she hears the words, instead of passing the potatoes his mother leaps up and hugs him.

Two weeks later when Mandy comes through the terminal and they go to lunch he has a surprise for her. He signs out: T-H-A-N-K Y-O-U F-O-R T-H-E C-A-R-D-S. I H-A-V-E B-E-E-N S-T-U-D-Y-I-N-G.

Mandy claps her hands to her chest and then leaps up and hugs Alfred. He never realized speaking other languages was good for so many hugs. He's going to have to study a lot more. She puts her hands on his shoulders and looks straight at him, still smiling. He doesn't see clouds in her eyes anymore. He only sees the most beautiful person he's ever encountered.

Mandy asks Alfred to her house for dinner. She's been living with her sister for the last year, since living alone finally became too challenging. That Saturday his father gives him a ride all the way up to Ballard, where Mandy's sister Laura has an apartment.

As Alfred unbuckles his seat belt and opens the car door his dad says, *I don't give a damn what your mother or the doctors say. This kind of thing is good for you, son. You go in there and be a gentleman, and you'll charm her right out of her knickers, as your grampaw used to say.* He says since they're all the way up here he's having a drink with an old friend. *See you at nine on the nose. Go get her!*

The dinner doesn't go so well. Mandy's older sister Laura is protective and doesn't think she should be hanging around with men these days, much less strangers from the airport. She doesn't say as much but Alfred can tell she's also thinking, *Much less* this *particular stranger.* It's the first time he's felt something come between him and Mandy, and it does a number on his nerves.

A few weeks later they go to his house for dinner and it doesn't go any better. His mother seems embarrassed and hardly says a word. His dad seems to think that he can cure deafness if only he yells loudly enough.

Alfred and Mandy stick to the airport for a while.

Months pass. The doctors and specialists and therapists say that Alfred is making much better progress but still hasn't eased back into the real world. The ear doctors in Los Angeles restore 10 percent of the hearing in Mandy's right ear but she still can't hear Alfred talking. Which is okay, because Alfred is nearly fluent in sign language by now.

After a while Alfred and Mandy start spending time together outside the airport. Laura comes to accept Alfred and sometimes they have movie nights at the apartment and Alfred sleeps on their couch. They go to Sea Fair and watch the Blue Angels. Alfred doesn't tell Mandy about the big house where he watched the Blue Angels and he doesn't tell her about the girl he barely remembers. They go to a Mariners game and to the museum and the library. After a while Mandy says Alfred can sleep in her bed with her. Alfred can tell that Laura, who otherwise seems to actually like him these days, *really* doesn't like that idea. Mandy tells her to butt out and, to Laura's credit, she does. Nothing happens between them in bed except they talk and sometimes cuddle before they fall asleep. Alfred discovers Mandy's bed is the safest place he's ever been. It's the only place where the accident and settlement don't linger at the edges of his thoughts. One night in Mandy's bed he dreams in French, and when they wake up the next morning he says, *Salut, jolie fille.*

Then one day Alfred sees Mandy at the airport and he knows something is wrong. They've gotten close and neither of them can keep a secret from the other. She walks up to him and throws her arms around him. She doesn't sign but says, *Laura and I are moving to Los Angeles. She got a job that pays double what she makes now and I can see the doctors twice a week instead of twice a month.*

Alfred doesn't understand why Mandy starts crying. He feels her tears soak through the shoulder of his shirt. After all, LA isn't so far. He tells her he can probably do the same job at LAX he's been doing at Sea-Tac. He's got loads of experience at this point. Most importantly, if it will make her hearing coming back faster he's all for it. Instead of comforting her it only makes her cry harder.

She says Laura is waiting outside and she has to go. She kisses him on the cheek and tells him they'll have him to dinner before they leave.

At dinner that weekend Mandy cries again and even Laura says how much she'll miss him. He tells them not to worry, he'll get a job at LAX and they can see each other all the time. After dinner they both hug him and tell him they'll write and call. He reminds them he'll be working at LAX soon.

Standing on the little walkway in front of Laura and Mandy's apartment Mandy tells Alfred she loves him. He says he loves her, too. He realizes they've never told each other that. He says, *Canit enim vobis cor meum,* which means, *My heart sings for you.*

It's the first time Mandy kisses Alfred on the lips. It's a real kiss, too. He kisses her back and when he closes his eyes he feels like he's back in her bed, in the safest place in the world. His mind explodes with thoughts in Latin, French, Italian, and languages he still doesn't recognize. Then she hugs him and is gone.

In the car his dad asks him if he's okay.

Alfred says, *Mi recorderó tutto per lei. I will remember everything for her.*

It's harder to get a job at LAX than Alfred thought it would be. Besides, the doctors and specialists and therapists say he's still easing back into the real world here in Seattle and moving to another city is out of the question, at least for now. It's best for him to stay at home until the easing in is finished. He feels a little frustrated but he tells himself he'll work even harder.

He does, and pretty soon he gets another job at the airport, one that comes with a paycheck and a timecard. He works on the grounds crew. He rides around with other employees in a white pickup with a bright orange light and a huge orange-and-white checkered flag in the back so taxiing planes are sure to see them. They look for objects on the taxiways and runways that could get sucked into a jet engine. He knows it's not the most glamorous job but it has the best perk he can imagine: he's getting paid to be driven around an active international airport and make sure the planes are safe. It's a part-time job and the rest of the time he still does his old job in the terminal.

He gets letters from Mandy every two weeks and sometimes she calls. She has a special phone that lets her hear pretty well, but the conversations aren't like the ones they had at the airport.

Alfred can almost feel the miles between them. She says she's going to visit. He's got three shoeboxes under his bed now, two filled with his earnings and one slowly filling with Mandy's letters. It's like keeping a little bit of their friendship for the future. With his languages coming back a little more and a little faster each day he knows it won't be long before he can write back to her.

He still has his Coca-Cola's at the airport shop, and the people who work there are as good to him as ever. He has his lunches at Red Robin, and sometimes he stays longer than his hour lunch break because there are so many people to talk to. His language is really coming back and people love to hear him speak in Italian, French, Spanish, German, and Latin. One day a Chinese couple come in and he amazes them by repeating their greeting, *Ni hao ma?* with flawless inflection, and by the time they hurry to their flight to Shanghai he's learned two dozen words in Mandarin. He even starts to learn to sign in his other languages and sometimes the airport managers ask him to help out. Every day he goes home with a few dollars in his pocket. He figures by the time he's eased back into the real world he'll have enough to go to LA. Maybe even enough to buy a house down there like the big one he had in Seattle.

In the terminal sometimes he sees a girl who looks like Mandy and he'll leap up. It's funny, he knows she's in Los Angeles, his memory is good enough these days that he can retain that fact, but a girl who looks like her makes him forget everything for a moment. But it's a nice kind of forgetting because the next second he remembers she's getting her ears back and that's what matters. He doesn't care if it takes one year or a hundred. They'll fix her ears one day and one day he'll ease back into the real world.

In the meantime the airport needs him, and he needs it.

A Jumbo Jet's Soul

When lightning blasted her nest she built it again on the same tree, in the splinters of the thunderbolt.
—Robinson Jeffers, The Beaks of Eagles

From the old pool chair in the backyard grass Daisy watches a jumbo jet lumber across the Los Angeles sky. *It's early autumn and the air is impossibly blue,* she thinks, then giggles when she hears Dorothea scold, *You can do better than that tired old cliché.*

As always she'd be right. Dorothea was Daisy's English teacher in her senior year at John Adams High School in Bakersfield. She was the one who convinced Daisy at the tender age of seventeen that she was destined to be a great literary writer. She was also Daisy's first true love.

After high school Daisy went to UC Davis, where it happened Dorothea was getting an MFA in creative writing. A few weeks into Daisy's sophomore year her favorite band played a concert down at the Sacramento Valley Amphitheater. The Jane's Addiction Show was the first of many road trips Daisy took with her roommate Eliza and two other girlfriends, and that night was also the first time any of them tried hallucinogens. As Daisy's mushroom trip peaked in an explosion of colors and Roman candles above the stage where the band was belting out the psychedelic "Three Days," she twirled straight into Dorothea's—at that moment they were still Ms. Creasy's—arms. Something other than the shrooms, something cosmic and beautifully inexplicable fueled by music and autumn sunset, inspired her to kiss her former teacher full on the lips. Ms. Creasy reciprocated tentatively at first before cupping Daisy's cheeks and kissing her more passionately than anyone ever had, boy or girl. By the end of the song Ms. Creasy was Dorothea. By the end of the concert Dorothea was Tia.

Tia kept Daisy sane through the mind-numbing modern college experience, and as much out of desperation to be finished and get on with life as aptitude for her studies Daisy graduated in three years. They moved to Los Angeles and rented a three-bedroom ranch-style house in Mar Vista, an up-and-coming section of the westside that, before yuppies started moving, in was called *that sketchy area between Venice and Culver City.* They rescued a Jack Russell Terrier mix and named him Davey, after the Jane's Addiction guitarist Dave Navarro. Tia helped Daisy swap Craptastic Sam, the fifteen-year-old Honda Civic her parents bought her in high school, for a slightly used Subaru Outback. The three of them went camping nearly every weekend in the spring and summer. The eastern Sierras, Owens Valley, Sana Ynez, even as far north as the Trinity Alps. Daisy had never seen so much of her home state before Tia. For two years she was as happy as she had been in her life. They proposed to each other an even dozen times, each time getting a little more serious about it.

Then Daisy's writing career took off and Tia's didn't. Daisy got a job with *LA Weekly* and Tia drifted. Daisy's fiction was published in literary journals and she started working on her first novel. Tia worked part-time at the local indie bookstore and started drinking. Daisy started doing yoga and became a vegan. Tia stopped exercising altogether and became an alcoholic. By their fourth year together Daisy's best friend, teacher, and lover was slipping away from her. Daisy didn't know whether the alcohol was changing Tia or if the woman she loved was a different person than she'd thought. They spent the last two years of their life together in a sort of living purgatory in which Daisy's happiness was inversely proportionate to the amount of booze Tia had consumed on any given day. When it came, the agonizing decision was a relief.

Their last night together they made love, agreeing without saying that maybe just maybe it would produce one last spark of the old magic. In the beginning they'd been able to turn each other on with a sideways glance across a crowded room. They'd read each other's minds and bodies to a degree that was downright uncanny, like the night at Manny's party in WeHo when they made eye contact in the living room and ninety seconds later were in the car, windows down, on their way to Dan Tana's for martinis and steak. Once they were out of earshot of anyone lingering in Manny's manicured front yard they shouted simultaneously, *Dan Tana's steaks, nightcap at Formosa, home to fuck!* They laughed halfway to the restaurant and Daisy never felt more in love. The last night, as she slid her hands along the familiar curve of Tia's hips she'd thought, if not the magic, at least a soft-sweet last memory. An hour later Tia smashed their coffee pot on the floor, snatched her bottle of Stoli from the freezer (spilling three bags of Whole Foods frozen peas on the kitchen floor, the remnants of which Daisy was still discovering months later and breaking down every time) and peeled out of the driveway of the place that suddenly wasn't home anymore. Five hours later, at two in the morning, two cops knocked on the door. They told Daisy that Tia had downed the bottle and gone off the road on Mulholland Drive a half mile south of Coldwater, which was about the worst stretch of the worst road she could have picked for that particular wrong turn. Her green Honda CR-V plunged 150 feet into a ravine and all the airbags in Detroit wouldn't have saved Dorothea Creasy. Daisy didn't attend the funeral in Tia's hometown of Braintree, Massachusetts because Tia had never told her family she was a lesbian.

Now Daisy watches the plane, studies it. She drags on a Marlboro and thinks it's one of those new superjumbos. An Airbus, maybe, or Lockheed. Lockheed still makes jumbo jets, right? As it sweeps with a white noise whisper across the LA basin she sees it's one of the double-deck jobs and she knows it's an Airbus because it was all over the news when the first one touched down at LAX last year. Biggest passenger jet in the world, she seems to recall reading it can carry 700 people. The jet seems aware of its size, something in its angle of attack suggesting to Daisy that it knows of the absurdity of something as big as itself carrying so many people through the sky at nearly the speed of sound. *It's almost apologetic*, she thinks, *and why not?* It *is* absurd, but not because it seems to defy logic and maybe even physics but because of its very necessity. In one hundred years humanity has gone from the last horses and buggies and first coughing Model T's to whisking itself around by the hundreds at 35,000 feet and 600 miles per hour. That's the absurdity the plane wears as visibly as its Air Emirates livery, she's certain of it.

Then she thinks, *You're certain of that sort of idea because it's your own. You'll never tell anyone about it and so it will never be challenged or worse, laughed at. Though there was a time not so long ago you'd have told Tia, and a time not long before that when she'd have kissed you and said,* Write that down, baby, before you forget it. It's beautiful. *Oh yes, you'd have told that haunted face. You'd have told her everything. And you did, didn't you?*

Like the fact that you'd fucked Manny. It seemed like a good idea to come clean. You thought you owed her at least that, in spite of everything. And you felt so righteous. Deep down you also thought she'd forgive you. No, you expected *her to forgive you. She'd inflicted so much pain on you and you'd forgiven her so many times, and finally you gave as good as you got. Well, you've seen how that worked out, Daisy girl. An eye for an eye and the whole world goes blind, as they say.*

Do you remember lying in her arms, both of you knowing it was the last time and this time probably forever, if not then certainly for a good long time? Of course you do. You remember how you just wanted to make those final few moments last, stretch them out and taste them like carnival taffy. So why did you do it? Was it because you thought if she forgave you, you guys would somehow be even? No, it was because you wanted to finish the thing. You wanted to be certain, this time. After four years of uncertainty and two years of hell, you were exhausted. Besides, you figured Manny's queer too so it didn't really count.

Daze, you old rationalizer, you.

Actually, Daisy thinks as the plane begins its gentle bank toward LAX, *maybe the only things any of us is ever certain about are the things we don't tell anyone. Like how I'll never share my belief that a 750,000 pound jumbo jet has a soul. Or like how I didn't tell Tia why I slept with Manny. If I'd told her she would have protested, I can hear her,* Oh, Daze, can't you see why you did it? *And I would have seen and then there would have been no certainty about anything.*

And so I didn't tell Tia the why, just like I'll never tell Manny the afterward. No, I can't tell him that (even Tia would have agreed with that part). I'm certain of my choice and I'm certain of the reasons behind it. Manny is like Tia was before the booze got both its hands on her. If I told him he'd say, Oh, Daze, we can't do that! *Yes, he'd have said we just like Tia always did, and that would be the problem. It's not we, Manny, it's me. You're a good man but you're good to a fault.*

As the jet fades to a point of light Daisy resolves not to tell anyone about the jumbo jet's soul. She'll keep it secret, too. Just as she won't tell Manny about her choice, and just as she didn't tell Tia the why behind her affair.

A small business jet passes low overhead and banks sharply north toward Santa Monica Airport. It seems much more at home in the sky than the jumbo jet. She remembers suddenly that she'd heard a jet pass low over the house when she was standing in the living room with Tia's still-beating heart on the floor at her feet, watching her love rampage through the kitchen and thinking, *I'm not stopping you, am I? You're smashing the things we bought together and I'm not stopping you. Can't you see, goddamnit? Can't you see and just fucking leave?*

Ever occur to you she might have heard you loud and clear? Ever think maybe she was making her own kind of certainty? No, you've just assumed she was in a blind rage because you'd ripped her heart out and she was half in the bag. A bull dyke in a China shop. But maybe she was sending her own message, and you were the one who missed it. Maybe—

But that's where we stop, isn't it Daisy old gal? We don't let ourselves go into that particular place, do we? No-ho, we don't. We've walled it up with bricks and mortar like Fortunato (hoping like Hell he doesn't start hollering and shaking his chains, because then our psyche would be really fucked). Let's keep it that way for now, shall we?

Besides, she thinks, *you have more pressing issues.*

It makes her feel better, in a way, knowing that even the mightiest jumbo jet might, just might, have a conscience and a soul. That it just might be able to see the world through the eyes of the tiny human beings that are its charge. It's reassuring because it means maybe we're not alone. Maybe we're all connected, maybe there's an energy that runs through even the warm hydraulic veins of the world's biggest flying machine.

It makes her feel better, this certainty. It's the kind of thought that will make tomorrow a little bit easier, and the days and months to come after it. She'll be alone but she won't be. All she'll have to do is look up in the sky to know.

Clouds of Men

I'm gonna get lit up when the lights go up in London
I'm gonna get lit up as I've never been before
You will find me on the tile
You'll find me wreathed in smiles
I'm gonna get so lit up I'll be visible for miles

I can hear a thousand things at once.

Amazing, really.

I can hear it all.

Every sound.

There are sounds at 22,000 feet you'd never imagine.

I didn't.

My mask is on.

I'm breathing.

Helmet's loose for a minute.

Gloves on.

Always, always keep your gloves on at altitude.

Even if.

The air is ice crystals, and I hear them, too.

Never noticed.

Simon's in the glass house.

Machinegun Kelly.

Give 'em Hell, Simon.

Sit up.

Sit. up.

Sit. Up.

Pete took my ammo box.

Make with the bullets, Benny

Flak was bad on this run.

Bad's we've seen.

Could get out and walk on it.

Fort took a direct hit a hundred yards away.

Dear Christ I hope I never see that again as long as I live.

Don't want to look at the ball turret.

Don't want to look at Andy.

Sit up.

Andy's a good gunner.

Was a good gunner.

Is, was, they don't matter up here.

Should but don't.

Make with the bullets, Benny

I'm gonna get lit up when the lights go up in London

Thing I didn't appreciate is how frail we are at 22,000 feet.

How could I?

In the Quonset we say, *We're gonna bring Hell.* Righteous fire.

We say it in the pubs and restaurants. The cafés, too.

Raindrops on the roofs, we said.

Righteous fire.

I'm gonna get so lit up I'll be visible for miles

On the ground Marvelous Meryl looks like Hell waiting to be brought.

Put another nail in Hitler's coffin.

The kids from the village think it's the greatest thing:

Marvelous Meryl's four engines spittin' fire and twelve crew pissin' acid

We give them candy and little flags and spent shell casings.

They wave when we take off.

I'm gonna get lit up when the lights go up in London
I'm gonna get lit up as I've never been before
You will find me on the tile
You'll find me wreathed in smiles
I'm gonna get so lit up I'll be visible for miles

They wave.

Been bringin' Hell almost six months now.

Bringin' Hell 7,000 pounds at a time.

Twenty-two missions.

Two-three hundred Forts per sortie.

Once there were a thousand bombers.

Imagine the Hell we've brought.

Make with the bullets, Benny

I got six confirmed.

More like fifteen, but who's counting.

Some things you don't boast about.

Fate has good ears up here.

(There's four more, coming out of the sun)

(Watch 'em)

I can hear a thousand things.

I can hear the airplane.

I think she's as scared as we are.

I'm gonna get lit up when the lights go up in London

I'm gonna get lit up as

Sons of bitches.

Son of a bitch Hun sons of bitches.

In gunnery school we learned not to shout on the intercoms.

Strange to hear, I'm hit, I think I'm done, like a weather report.

Stranger still, *B-17 out of control, three o'clock*

Calm as an Essex sunset,

C'mon you guys, get out of that plane, bail out

There's one, he came out of the bomb bay

Yeah, I see 'em

There's the tail gunner coming out

That's Joey for sure

(Watch out for fighters)

See any parachutes, Pete

Come on, guys

There's three

Four

Five

Six

(Watch out for fighters)

Six left inside

Come on get out of there

Now damn it

Goddamn it get the Hell out get out get out get out

That's it

All right cut the chatter

Watch out for fighters

There's nothing heroic in it, nothing desperate.

I said, Cap'n, left waist down, like I was ordering coffee.

Quiet as a Kansas afternoon amid the thousand sounds.

Cap'n, left waist down

Said the radioman to the gunner

Well how are we fixed for lead

I'm gonna get lit up when the lights go up in London

I hate Messerschmitts.

Hate them to goddamn Hell.

Two second bursts, don't hold the trigger

But this time I saw his eyes.

I held the trigger.

I had to.

Because I saw his eyes.

They were smiling.

He was smiling.

> *see me wreathed in smiles*

You don't smile when you're killing Marvelous Meryl.

When you kill Andy in the ball turret.

When you're trying to kill me.

(Watch out for fighters)

I blew it because of his eyes.

And now I can feel the air.

At 22,000 it feels so very lonely.

My legs don't work.

> *I'll be visible for miles*

It smells like cordite.

Oil and asbestos.

Something else, too.

Meryl's as afraid as we are.

(That got him, he's smoking)

Hang in there, girl.

Hang in there.
Cap'n'll get us home.

Simon's still shooting.
Give 'em Hell, Simon.
Tailgunner Drew's out of ammo.
Best card shark in the squadron.
Won us plenty.
Counts cards.
How's that work?
(Watch out for fighters)
How's any of it work.
Never wondered.
War's the strangest thing.
Hadn't thought about it.
You don't until you have time.
There's time at 22,000 feet.

We do what has to be done.
That's all there is.

He saw the target and locked the target
And suddenly bombs away
(Black smoke black smoke)
(That's a good hit)
(Good run)
(Flak's stopped again)
(Watch for fighters)

I'm at that strange brink.

I could imagine myself back to the farm.

That would do it.

I'd cry, for sure.

(Here they come)

(Two o'clock I see 'em)

(I've got about a hundred rounds left)

(Chose your shot)

(Three more coming from twelve o'clock high)

(They got Pete)

(Pete)

Don't lie yet.

Could be on the farm.

In my room with my brother James.

Don't lie.

I could be in Mama's arms.

Don't lie.

I'd cry into Mama's arms.

Autumn Kansas sun is like warm melted butter.

Warm.

The adrenaline's off.

Cold through my jacket.

Cold in this bomber.

That means something.

When it gets cold.

Cap'n, we're bad back here.

I know. Hang on, Johnny. Twenty-five minutes.

I'll hear a thousand things in twenty-five minutes.

Cap'n's talking to the other planes.

Make with the bullets, Benny.

I can hear them, too.

Out of a thousand sounds, the bombers.

Said the bombardier to the pilot

Call it a day, and then

Sit up.

Sit the Hell up.

We're making the turn, now.

Means we're past Belgium.

Make believe little country.

Supposed to prevent all of this.

Lot of good Belgium did for Andy.

Fat lot of good Belgium did for Pete.

I'm gonna get lit up when the lights go up in London

There's our halo on a cloud.

Blessed Meryl.

Blessed be.

Sometimes a Fort looks like a cross.

Something in that.

Reminds me:

O most merciful

O most merciful

Jesus wash my blood in the sins

Wash my sins in blood

I live for thee

Amen

Can't remember.

Hell of a time to forget.

Pete's got one hand on his .50.

God bless him.

Andy, too.

     They lived for thee

Don't know if Andy's still there.

They lived for thee

     the bombers

Johnny

Yeah, I think. *Yeah, Johnny.*

Sun's out.

Now we're clear for sure.
Damn that feels good.

The weather's fine for flying
The fog has gone to bed
There's such good visibility
You can see victory ahead

No foolin' Johnny
No foolin', Cap'n. I'm all right.
    I am all right.
        I am all right.
            I'm doin' just fine.

I'm gonna get lit up

Let's fill the air with eagles
Let's fill the clouds with men

It's beautiful up here, when the air isn't trying to kill you.

It's beautiful, the blue,
    and I hear a thousand things.
        Meryl's halo on the white clouds.
Singing
    fill the air with eagles

We're descending.

Meryl will descend.

Pete will descend.

So will Andy.

Simon.

Me.

Maybe the Cap'n.

      We'll descend

          then climb.

There's the cliffs.

Good.

Rest.

Let's fill the air with eagles
Let's fill the clouds with men

        And we shall see a world that's free

            When we fly home again

Johnny you're gonna make it

Damn right, skipper.

I'm pissin' acid.

      Let's fill the air with eagles
      Let's fill the clouds with men

         a thousand things at once

the beginning and end

my heart beat

Let's fill the clouds with men

(Stagecoach Nine turning final)
(We've got five wounded souls aboard)
(Clear the field clear the field he's going to belly in)
(Stagecoach Nine field is yours)
(Godspeed fellas)

lead the target two seconds

my heart
beat

Mama

the bombers   *Mama*

watch for fighters
watch his eyes
visible for miles

for thee
the bombers

for thee

clouds of men

it's me Mama

home again

(going to help you, son)

home again

clouds of men

clouds of men

The Orange
(with a Kandy Kim fly-by)

Ah, Hell. We had more fun in a week than those weenies had in a lifetime.
—*Florence "Pancho" Barnes*

Here we pause to note that the hero of our next story, Colonel Charlie "Chance" Rashad, United States Air Force (retired) only told his tale three times. The first time he told it was to his wife, Lynnette, who took it as though it was the most natural thing in the world and actually thought it was pretty neat. The second time was when he told their daughters. Monica, who would grow up to be an astronomer and an associate professor at Cal Tech, was not particularly impressed. Chelsea, on the other hand, said her dad's stories were one of the main reasons she became a fighter pilot herself.

The third telling was a little more involved. Chance retired from the Air Force a Colonel at the age of fifty-three. He could have gone for General but there was no flying in it. Hell, there'd barely been enough flying in Colonel to keep him interested. In their retirement years he and Lynnette did a lot of flying and a lot of camping and fishing. They went mostly to Idaho, Wyoming, and Montana but they also took trips to British Columbia and Alaska. One of their favorite stops in Alaska was the town of Yakutat on the Kenai Peninsula. They'd always stay a couple nights at the Yakutat Inn, a hotel, bar, and diner situated on a corner of the field at Yakutat Airport a stone's throw from Monti Bay. No one could recall who built the two-story log cabin with a little porch in front where you could have a beer and watch airplanes (or more accurately look at airplanes, since Yakutat Airport isn't exactly JFK) and a deck in the back where you could watch the waves crash on the rocks in the bay and hear the gulf wind rustle the pines. If you're lucky you'll spot a pod of orca, and if you're especially fortunate a herd of humpback whales migrating like the sea itself. The inn's origins were mysterious, but outside the king salmon in Kodiak there's no better place to hear flying stories. As a result, one of Chance and Lynette's nights at the Inn invariably culminated in a Bacchanalia of storytelling, drinking, and shooting pool with local fishermen, bush pilots, and barflies.

One night last spring the regulars (among whom Chance and Lynette came to count themselves) were joined by a pair of oddly dressed fellows who both stood more than six-six and looked like brothers, the only difference being that one had a bushy red beard with a few strands of white in it and the other had a bushy gray beard with a few strands of red remaining. They looked like lumberjacks but it turned out they were brother pilots and writers.

They were hail-fellows-well-met and within an hour everyone was delightfully drunk and an expert pool shot.

Stories were swapped, several tall tales grew a couple inches, and eventually the conversation came around to the strangers—whose names were Filnik and Borse, or Red Beard and White Beard depending on how many drinks you'd had—and how they'd come to be in Yakutat.

The fellows told stories about Kandy Kim along with a few other stories about airplanes behaving in mysterious and possibly supernatural ways. They inquired about Derringer Bill to no avail. Chance and several of the bush pilots had heard of Kandy Kim, but until that night at the Yakutat Inn they'd assumed the stories were legends. When Filnik and Borse confirmed she was in fact quite real seven of the bush pilots, along with a retired Delta Airlines 747 captain named Trent Wilcox, volunteered on the spot to help with the reclamation. Captain Wilcox and four of the bush pilots were sober enough the following morning to join the fellows on the glacier. Captain Wilcox and two of them later became full fellows, the first Americans to gain the distinction. The honors were bestowed in a complex and wonderfully dangerous wing-walking ceremony over the Labrador Coast.

That night at the Yakutat Inn it might have been the booze or the cast of characters, it might have been the camaraderie or the fact that Chance and Lynette were 2,000 miles from home in an Alaskan saloon with a bunch of bush pilots and a wayward jumbo jet captain. Whatever the reason, the more Chance talked to Filnik and Borse the more he realized, the more he knew in his very soul, that they needed to hear his tale. It was a flying story but he believed it had a deeper significance. For the first time he was in the company of people who maybe could help him find it.

The evening had started with ale and games of Nine-Ball, progressed to gin and Eight-Ball, then reached a crescendo during the Ballad of Kandy Kim with bourbon and Snooker. By the time the Ballad was done a sort of benevolent calm had descended upon the room, and upon Chance and Lynette and the fellows, and the barkeep, and the dozen other pilots and barflies. They heard waves crashing on the rocks and the big Alaska wind in the trees. Outside the front window the three-quarter moon made the planes on the ramp glow. The barkeep walked to the fireplace and lit a small blaze more for ambiance than warmth. There were contented sighs. It was the kind of night that called for a fire.

When everyone had had some time alone with their thoughts, Chance got up and ordered a round of India Pale Ales for the room and handed the barkeep some money. The barkeep made some change and handed back to him a larger amount than Chance had started off with. Chance took a few more bills out of his pocket, slapped the entire amount on the bar and said with a slight slur, *And there's a little somepin' extra for you.*

The transaction thus consummated and the ales passed 'round, Chance leaned against the fireplace mantle beneath a big wood-framed black-and-white of a Cessna 185 float plane flying past Denali. He figured standing gave him a better shot of making it through his story without passing out, which was becoming a decided possibility. But he also knew his story would keep everyone else wide, wide awake.

Chance tapped his glass with his Air Force Academy ring and the room fell quiet. He said, *I've never seen an airplane fly itself, less'n you count drones—and dammit, I do not count drones. There were a few good-natured Here, here's!*

Chance continued, *I never saw one, but I heard stories along those lines during my career and I never had reason to doubt 'em. In fact, part of me kind of clung to them, if you know what I mean. But I've never heard anything quite like that ballad you just wove for us. Thank you.* He raised his bottle, *To Kandy Kim!*

The room boomed, *To Kandy Kim!*

Bottles and glasses were clinked, huzzahs exchanged. There were handshakes and fist bumps. Someone put some money in the jukebox and played a song called "The Pilot" by a singer (who happened to be a fellow, but the fellows kept that to themselves) who called himself the White Buffalo.

When the song ended, Chance continued. *I haven't seen an airplane fly itself, but I've seen something I couldn't explain. It's how I know every word of your story about Kandy Kim is true. I know you fellows will enjoy hearing what happened over the Mojave Desert in 1983. That was the first time it happened, anyway, but I'm getting ahead of myself.*

Now listen here…

C<small>R</small>

SURE ENOUGH THE ROOM hung on his every word and peppered him with questions when he was through. Filnik in particular loved Chance's story. He kept slapping his knee and punching his brother in the shoulder and shouting, *Yes, yes, of course!* He pounded the table so hard it cracked down the middle. You can see the cracked table to this day if you're ever in the Yakutat Inn.

When Chance was done with his story both Filnik and Borse were weeping. Not because it was a sad story, but because it moved them to their cores. The fellows are like that. A good story well told, much less one about airplanes, is something akin to a religious experience for them. Besides, they're a pretty emotional bunch to begin with. The fact that this Colonel was favoring them with one after keeping it within his family so long made it that much more special, like a bottle of fine wine that's been aging in the cellar awaiting the perfect occasion to be opened and shared.

Which is an apt simile, because ever since the night when Filnik and Borse happened to be in the Yakutat Inn at the same time as a retired Air Force Colonel named Chance and everyone got drunker than they thought humanly possible, it's been a tradition to quaff round after round and retell their stories. As you might have guessed, the stories don't change much. Even the chattiest pilots, the ones who can't resist cracking bad jokes on the radio when they're stacked up over O'Hare, fall into a sort of reverent silence the first time they hear the stories.

Which is one of the magical aspects of aviation: hallowed ground is everywhere, places where great pilots have lived and flown and told their tales. Some of those places are obvious, like Kitty Hawk or the ruins of Pancho Barnes' Happy Bottom Riding Club near Edwards Air Force Base in the Mojave Desert. Others, like the saloon at the Yakutat Inn where Chance Rashad and Filnik and Borse first told their stories, where bush pilots have spun yarns for damn near one hundred years, are hidden. People fly in search of them. In fact that search is the reason a lot of pilots became pilots in the first place.

Incidentally, the story of the giant orange is also, in a roundabout way, how the Ballad of Kandy Kim found its way to us, and how this little volume of flying stories came to be in your hands.

ଦ୍ୟ

THE FIRST TIME COLONEL Charlie "Chance" Rashad saw it he was still in flight school. He was two weeks from graduation and flying a routine navigation exercise over the China Lake Weapons Range in the Mojave Desert on a July morning in 1983. He was part of a four-ship flight of T-38 Talon advanced trainers. The Talon is a supersonic, twin-engine bullet that's essentially a stripped-down jet fighter. The day's mission was a combat navigation practice in which he would separate from his wingmen and shut off his avionics and radios to simulate a failure. The objective was to use visual aids to get back to his squadron and get back home.

He started off in formation at 32,000 feet at 0800 hours. The instructor, Major Sam "Trigger" Tillwell, called, *OK, Arc Light Three, break. Arc Light flight, turn left heading one-one-zero, follow my lead. 'Luck, Arc Light Three.*

Chance toggled his mic. *Arc Light Three, on the break. See you at happy hour.*

Chance kicked his Talon into a five-g break and dove for the ground at 450 knots. His squadron mates streaked away in a flash of silver at a combined 800 knots.

Not that Chance was watching.

He focused on the desert floor rushing at him. The azure of 32,000 feet gave way to the pale blue of the sea level morning. He leveled off at 500 feet and the earth righted itself. The plane had hair trigger controls, Chance took a deep breath and it breathed with him. Chance banked steep left around a bald hilltop and a cluster of joshua trees blurred past a hundred feet from his helmet. He reversed the turn, firewalled the throttles, and punched the plane out to the middle of the desert.

Chance had a habit of singing while he flew. It was an unconscious habit and the songs usually related to whatever he was doing. Flying over the desert at near the speed of sound, he hummed Billy Joel's "The Ballad of Billy the Kid."

Well, he never traveled heavy

Yes, he always rode alone

And he soon put many older guns to shame...

He was humming the bridge when one of the controllers back at Edwards, simulating the role of the E-3 AWACS command plane, called, *Arc Light flight, Arc Light flight, this is Grand Central. We've lost radio and radar contact with Arc Light Three. Advise, over.*

That was the signal for Chance to shut off his radios and avionics. He flipped the switches and his screen and earphones went dead. He was now flying blind. And he loved it. In an era when every square foot of earth had been mapped, when airspace was monitored by radar and the new satellite global positioning systems and linked by a billion devices, where flying was increasingly a matter of autopilots, computers, checklists, protocols, and paperwork, pilots flew for the few minutes every once in a blue moon when it would be just them and the machine. In Chance's case, he had a few minutes alone with a supersonic Air Force trainer.

While the rest of Arc Light flight maneuvered to their start place on the other side of the desert, Chance lit the Talon's afterburners and flipped inverted. Just because. The desert floor zoomed over his head 500 feet below. At the crest of a sandstone arroyo he stood the plane on its right wing, pulled his power and dove into a canyon at 350 knots.

This was Mach Canyon, a twelve-mile-long, quarter-mile-wide, and half-mile-deep natural sandstone drag strip for fighter pilots. At the eight-mile point the canyon doglegged to the south. The 2,000-foot wall at the turn was called the Ramp. In violation of about one hundred regulations fliers played chicken with the Ramp, and there were even a few black marks across its face from particularly close runs by F-15, F-16, and T-38 pilots. Airplane junkies set up campsites on the rim above the Ramp and filmed the planes.

Chance pushed the Talon fifty feet closer to the canyon floor, low enough that he could see individual spikes on the joshua trees. Over his shoulder his airplane's shadow kept formation on the canyon wall.

The trick to the Ramp was the skid. You approached high enough and slow enough to safely make the six-g turn but low enough and fast enough to tag the Ramp. Tricky enough in a

Viper with 30,000 pounds of thrust or an Eagle with twice that, carrying no weapons and with half tanks. The Talon was a high-performance jet but it maxed out at 9,000 pounds of thrust and when you pulled more than seven g's you were on your own, pal.

But the plane felt good today, so Chance set himself up for the run. Out of the corner of one eye he saw tents, tripods, and people on the ridge. He was singing louder.

> *Well, he robbed his way from Utah to Oklahoma*
> *And the law just could not seem to track him down.*
> *And it served his legend well,*
> *For the folks, they loved to tell,*
> *'Bout when Billy the Kid came to town...*

Two thousand feet from the Ramp he pointed the nose at the horizon, let eighty knots bleed off his airspeed then lit his afterburners and pulled the plane into a perfect 70-degree right turn. The HUD said 7.2g's and he held it there for a few seconds until he felt the buffeting of ground effect from the face of the Ramp. He eased off the turn, pushed the nose down, and leveled off with a precise snap at 400 feet AGL and 290 knots, increasing quickly, down the last four miles of Mach Canyon. He looked over his shoulder and saw people waving and jumping.

He shouted out loud, *Whoo-haah! I love this shit!*

As he started to climb he hummed *Fly Me to the Moon.* Checked the clock, they'd be in position in ninety seconds. *And here I be*, he thought, ahead of schedule as per. He climbed out of the canyon and glanced at the avionics out checklist. He pretended to cycle the systems, going through the procedure with his gloved hand. OK, no dice, time for a little dead reckoning. He hummed the second verse and started an ascending left turn to set up the—

Which is when he noticed he had a wingman. Or rather, a wing-something. It was an orange. Not literally an orange, but an orange was the only earthly thing Chance could think of. About five times the size of his Talon, it was keeping pace with his jet as if it was the most natural thing in the world. He couldn't see any canopy or windows, in fact he could not make out any flight surfaces at all. It was—well, it was a giant flying orange.

He flipped the dark sun visor down on his helmet. For some reason it made him feel better, like a kid who knows his Star Wars sheets will protect him from the monsters under his bed. Which was an apt analogy, because the giant orange flying next to his jet on an otherwise beautiful day in the desert pretty well reduced him to childlike mental processes. It happens to all of us at one time or another, when something happens that's so big we just sort of revert to the fundamentals. In Chance's case, the fundamentals involved keeping a jet in the air. He kept singing, consciously now, to calm himself.

> *Fill my heart with song,*
> *And let me sing forevermore.*
> *You are all I long for,*
> *All I worship, and adore.*
> *In other words, what the fuck?*
> *In other words, WHAT THE FUCK?!*

They'd climbed to 5,000 feet and leveled off. Chance gently brought the Talon into a shallow right turn (again, like the kid under the blanket who when his arm falls asleep shifts very, very slowly so's not to wake the monsters). The orange followed along, and as they turned it started to bob up and down next to him. It did it slowly at first, increasing until it was a blur. After a few seconds it stopped bobbing and hung in space off his wing.

Something (he would never be able to say what that something was) told him the orange expected him to mirror its maneuver. Chance said to the cockpit, *Why not? I mean, what could possibly go wrong?*

He repeated the maneuver, somewhere in the back of his addled mind enjoying the rollercoaster effect of positive and negative g's in the light, nimble aircraft. After a dozen or so, he returned to the turn. Which, he realized, was now a formation maneuver.

After they mirrored the bobbing maneuver, the giant orange performed the first of many maneuvers Chance would never be able to explain. It zipped out in front of him, accelerating from 320 knots to what he figured was somewhere in the vicinity of light speed, stopped dead, then shot to the right across his flight path, turned 90 degrees again and shot past him on the right. He looked over his shoulder and saw the orange repeat the maneuver behind him, and a half-second later it resumed its position off his left wing, bobbing contentedly.

So the giant orange wanted a flying contest. Chance actually shrugged. He shook his head and said, *I'm afraid this isn't going to be too impressive compared to your nine hundred g maneuvers there. But here goes.*

He barrel rolled right, then barrel rolled left. The orange bobbed. He snap-rolled left, and snap-rolled right. The orange bobbed a little more. He lit the 'burners and flew a high-performance (relatively-speaking) loop, then an inverted loop. The orange bobbed more quickly.

Then it streaked away. It zipped ahead at mach insanity as before, paused, then shot straight into the sky and was gone. Chance checked the clock. The whole incident had lasted less than ninety seconds. He shook his head a couple times, brought the Talon level at 5,000, and restarted his exercise checklist.

Chance didn't mention the orange at happy hour, and left it out of his post-flight debrief and report.

Chance saw the orange from time to time over the years. He graduated at the top of his class and became an F-15 driver, first in Nevada, then Alaska, and later in Germany and the Middle East. He flew in both gulf wars.

The second time he saw the orange he was on a ferry flight from Nellis Air Force Base to Reykjavik, Iceland, for an annual NATO exercise. The biggest challenges on the flight were staying awake and figuring out different ways to keep your ass cheeks from falling asleep. Nine fighters were stretched out in a loose formation over a mile. Icebergs spiked the blue north Atlantic and the flight slipped in and out of clouds.

He was puttering with a nav control when the orange appeared off his right wing. It bobbed hello. As if he'd learned it in flight school (which he kind of did, he reflected) he bobbed back. This time it performed the maneuvers he had done five years ago in the Talon. Only this time Chance couldn't do anything remotely like them. He was slinging three 610 USGAL external tanks under his belly and wings, and another 850 gallons on each side of his fuselage in conformal fuel tanks. Ferry configuration, otherwise known as the flying elephant. Plus he didn't have the extra fuel for afterburners. The orange finished the maneuvers, and then bobbed off his right wing.

Chance did a series of gentle turns, sweeping back and forth in a lazy eight. He inverted, but that was about it. He felt terrible.

The orange repeated his maneuvers, then did them a second time. Then it did the Talon maneuvers again and bobbed off his right wing. He sensed it was impatient. He keyed his mic, *Ah, Rosebud flight, Rosebud Two. Anyone else see a kind of orangish thing over in my direction, over?*

There were a few snickers from bored pilots, and two wingmen drifted over to look. But as soon as he keyed his mic, the orange shot straight up and disappeared.

No shit, he said into his mask.

His wingman said, *Rosebud Two, Rosebud Five, Negative on the orangish-thingy.*

Another chimed in, *Rosebud Two, Rosebud Seven, Ah, I got some white-ish thingies up here. Anyone else, over?*

Rosebud Seven, Rosebud Four, Affirmative on the white-ish thingies. I see some blue stuff, too, over.

Rosebud Seven, Rosebud Five, Ah, I've got bluish stuff above me and below me.

Someone who sounded liked Rosebud Lead called theatrically, *Everything is wrong. Everything looks strange, even the ocean!* It was a quote from Flight 19, the infamous Navy flight that vanished without a trace over the Bermuda Triangle in 1945.

Wiseasses, Chance mused. At least the chatter killed a few minutes.

The next time he saw the orange nearly broke his heart. He was in an F-15E Strike Eagle over Iraq on the first night of the Desert Storm air war. That night, when Iraqi defenses lit up the night sky and turned the air into shrapnel, he was coming off a bombing run when his plane took heavy anti-aircraft fire. It knocked out his left engine, tore into his wing, and wounded his Weapons Systems Officer, his backseater. The wounds weren't fatal but Lt. Trent "T-bone" Wilcox was in and out of consciousness. The only good news was the 120 mm rounds missed the conformal fuel tank. Another six inches back and Stagecoach 9 would have returned to earth in very small, very hot pieces.

He radioed his Mayday and limped toward Prince Sultan Air Base in Saudi Arabia. Before he landed he had to fly over the gulf and jettison his unspent ordinance. You didn't land a wounded plane with 10,000 pounds of bombs still hanging on it.

As they crossed the shoreline to the Gulf he toggled the intercom. *We'll be on the ground in ten minutes, T-bone. If you can hear me, click your 'com.*

Chance breathed a sigh of relief when the intercom clicked three times in his ears. Then T-bone said weakly, *Good goddamned flying back there, Chance. We ought to be dead right now.*

Thanks, partner. Save your strength. Drink some water if you can.

Roger that. Hey, Chance?

Yeah?

Good goddamned flying, but I'm still gonna kick your ass for getting me shot.

Hey, look on the bright side. Chicks dig Purple Hearts.

Then you should've gotten me shot before I got married, asshole.

Chance grinned into his oxygen mask. So long as T-bone had some piss and vinegar left in him he'd be fine. He glanced in the mirror on the canopy and saw that his wizzo's eyes were closed and he was breathing normally. Chance focused on getting his plane back to base. They'd cleared a lane for him back to Prince Sultan, and when he was five miles out they'd clear the pattern and runways. Piece of cake. He started humming "Hit the Road, Jack" by Ray Charles.

He saw the orange over the Gulf the moment before he hit the pickle and freed the ordinance. Its color was depleted and it didn't bob or do any impossible maneuvers. It didn't do much of anything. It hung in space a few hundred feet from Chance's dying plane. Even through the adrenaline and fear Chance felt a desperate, hopeless sadness. As it flew next to him it became dimmer still, nearly translucent. He could see the fires of Iraq in the distance through it. He watched it a long moment. He said, *I'm sorry.*

Then it was gone. With everything happening he couldn't tell if it zipped away as usual or just faded. As he dropped his bombs into the ocean he thought, *I wonder how often the universe is this disappointing.*

He didn't see the orange for many years after the war. At the end of his career he was given command of the 51st Air Wing in Honolulu, a kind of *thank you* gig for outgoing Colonels. Since he didn't play golf, to relax he sometimes rented a single-engine Beech Bonanza or Piper Malibu at Honolulu International and went island hopping. Sometimes Lynette joined him, sometimes he just went for a $400 hamburger on one of the other islands.

On an October afternoon with a few squalls lined up to the southeast and the sun preparing something extra in the west, Chance took off in a Beech Bonanza A36 from Lanai Airport after an early supper and flew low over the water looking for dolphins, or if he got lucky migrating gray or blue whales.

He overflew a small pod of bottlenose dolphins and banked to go around, pulling the throttle to descend and keeping the nose level to bleed airspeed. He'd just dropped 20 degrees of flaps and trimmed for ninety knots when the orange slid into formation off his right wing. It looked as it had the first two times. *If anything*, he thought as it pulled level, *it looked brighter*. This time he bobbed first, and he pushed the Bonanza into a few aggressive (relatively speaking) maneuvers.

When the orange started bobbing he had a thought. He dropped back toward the dolphin pod, slowing down again and dropping full flaps. He entered a slow, low circle at one hundred feet over the water and eighty knots. The orange followed his maneuvers and flight path and they circled above the dolphin pod.

He waited for the orange's next maneuver, but it remained in formation with him. They flew that way for a while, moving with the cetaceans. The orange drifted out of the turn and descended toward the water. The impossible maneuvers, the mere fact of the orange, paled in comparison to what happened next. It settled onto the surface of the water a bit in front of the dolphin pod. The water glowed orange and red like dye diffusing into the sea. When the dolphins entered the colors they started leaping and breaching into the air. The orange settled into the water until it was half submerged. The dolphins swam under it and leaped into it. They actually swam in it, and for the first time Chance realized the orange wasn't made of some futuristic space metal after all. It seemed to be pure light, pure energy. Chance found himself humming the theme song from Flipper. He chuckled to himself. Faster than lightning, indeed.

The orange rose from the water and came up next to him one more time. It was brighter than he'd ever seen it, almost too bright to look at directly. It seemed to pulse a little bit this time too. Chance was filled with the greatest sense of peace he'd ever known. He smiled and said to it, *Swimming with dolphins is pretty cool, huh?* The orange bobbed and shot into the sky. Back in the water the dolphins resumed their course, swimming lazily toward Lanai Island.

As he headed home to Honolulu he wondered if there might be a way to communicate with it. He thought maybe next time he'd try Morse, even a radio call. As the sun settled on the western rim of the Pacific Ocean he realized it was greedy to think like that. The orange is, and for him that's plenty. It renews his reverence for the sky. He set his course and enjoyed a few precious minutes alone with the plane. Unconsciously, he started singing.

> *Fly me to the moon,*
> *And let me play among the stars,*
> *Let me see what spring is like*
> *On Jupiter and Mars...*

Emergency Landing

It wasn't that Lester Morris didn't like people. In small doses in controlled environments he could find himself enthralled. Expressions, diction, dialects, inflection, tone. All of it was fascinating in a way. But in numbers, at the dinners his mother was fond of hosting, the card games his father played with other men in the parlor on Saturday afternoons, people overwhelmed him. They were unpredictable. They would turn on you in a heartbeat for reasons you'd never divine. One night Dad called him into the parlor and in front of a half dozen other men ordered him to recite the Pledge and the names of the presidents. They laughed when he got stuck at Grant. He stood for a solid minute while they watched (he could see the quivering at the corners of their mouths, the cruel amusement in their eyes) and said, *Grant...Grant...Grant. Then there was... Roosevelt?* The men had laughed harder and his father scolded them, out of embarrassment.

And school—oh, God, school! Chaos of bodies and voices, explosions of emotion and tomfoolery. The taunting (even when not directed at him) made him sick to his stomach. He was thin and, if one were being ungenerous, a frail and effete little boy (who would grow to be a thin and ungainly young man, tall and unsubstantial after adolescence wrought havoc on what little stone he did have). In America, in California, and especially in the new tracts in Riverside where he grew up, he wore those qualities like scarlet letters. The other boy like him, whose name was Danny Jackson, made himself clever to compensate for the things his body would never allow him to do. Try as he might Lester never made himself clever like Danny. He found the only way he could avoid the barbs of pubescent boys was to hide away. He sat for long hours at a cubbyhole desk in the school library playing with Chinese Checkers or puzzles or sometimes just staring into space. In high school the librarian was named Mrs. Brown and she was kind to him. He might have become a bookworm, only he rarely read books (they were full of characters, who were just people hiding behind some writer's brash efforts to clothe them in significance, and besides he never understood literary sleights of hand like symbolism and simile). He might have learned to be alone with his thoughts and maybe make something of them but Lester Morris was no more possessed of a facile mind than a robust physique. Elementary and high school were purgatories he hoped simply to survive.

For the first nineteen years of his life Lester also lived in the long shadow cast by his big brother, Chad. Which suited him just fine because Chad's shadow was an excellent place to hide.

When people in the neighborhood talked about *the Morris boy,* they always meant Chad. That was how they always said it, in the singular. Chad was a Boy Scout and then an Eagle Scout, he won the Pinewood Derby three years straight and earned more badges than any other boy in Riverside Circle. In high school he played three sports and as quarterback led the football team to state. For all his accomplishments, for all the attention and accolades that were heaped upon him, the only thing Chad ever wanted to do was fly airplanes. Chad's dream became Lester's dark obsession.

On a warm autumn morning in October, 1947 their dad gathered the family and two neighbors, Paul Kupfer the Democrat and Daryl Winstrom the Republican, at the glass and plastic table in the backyard. They all drank lemonade and Dad told them to watch the western sky because something big was about to happen. Like his older son William "Willy" Morris had grown up dreaming of airplanes. In the war he spent two years in the Army Air Corps bombing the Germans. He encouraged Chad's dreams with the sort of paternal dedication he would never direct at Lester.

The morning light had been hot, pale, and merciless. Lester heard voices and shouts from other yards. They were all watching. They watched the sky for what Lester felt must have been half the day but which was really less than a half-hour. Lester looked up at the crystalline expanse above them until his neck ached, all the while trying to follow the conversation. Whenever he lowered his head to rest his neck, Chad whispered, *You're gonna miss it, Rusty,* and Lester popped his head back up.

Paul said, *Yes, yes, son, you'll miss the DoD's spending of your national birthright on superfluities.* Lester saw Paul's left eye twitch unpleasantly, like a man who needs to break wind in the middle of a sermon.

Daryl said, *If your president hadn't ordered it and your congress hadn't appropriated it pretty soon Lester here wouldn't have any birthright to speak of. Isn't that right, my boy?*

Wanting to be done with it Lester said, *Yes, sir.*

Daryl said, *There's a good boy. Good to know at least one of the Morrises has his head screwed on straight.* He rustled Lester's hair and Lester shivered. He hoped it wasn't obvious. *Shut up, both of you. No politics today.*

Paul said again, *No, indeed, Willy, no politics on this our great day of national achievement. No politics in the way of millions of dollars on an aeroplane while Negros starve in Mississippi and Arkansas. Let's push forward the day of reckoning.*

So help me, Kupfer, I'll throw you out of my yard.

You and what army?

The adults went on arguing like that. Lester turned away from them. His stomach clenched. He hated when adults argued politics, hated even more when they used him as a bargaining chip.

The sky didn't change or give any hint of the great surprise Dad was talking about. Lester squinted and mixed the mountains and clouds and sky together in a kaleidoscopic whirl in which he hoped to find whatever it was they were supposed to see. He discovered nothing. He refocused his eyes and blinked in the sunlight.

Dad leapt up suddenly and pointed to the eastern mountains. *There he is!*

Four tiny white lines moved swiftly across the clear sky. When they were halfway across the horizon a fifth line appeared and streaked out in front of the others. Dad slapped Chad on the back and yelled *There he is! By God, look at him! He's going to make it, the old son of a bitch is going to make it!*

A few seconds later, a muted boom. Daryl shouted, *Wow! Didja hear that?*

There was whooping and cheering from the other yards, for Chuck Yeager had just broken the sound barrier in the rocket-powered Bell X-1. Daryl and Dad and Chad high fived. Lester strained but the words raced past like that white line, too fast to catch. He was silent. Paul took it as a sign of allegiance, looked over and winked. As if to say, *We know who's on the right side here.*

Chad gave him a high five. *What do you think about that, Rusty!*

Paul said, *The boy's too smart to be impressed by toys. Even ten million dollar toys.*

So help me, Paul. So help me.

You and what army?

Lester looked intently at the sky, like a man frowning at a car engine he knows nothing about. Dad and Chad did a funny dance. Daryl went into the house and came back with cans of beer.

Lester pondered what they'd seen. Lines in the sky, a boom, and now celebrations as the lines vanished and passed beyond the east hills. Chad gave him a bear hug. *Rusty, that boom means that a man went faster than anyone's ever gone before.*

More confused than ever Lester had asked, *What's he doing way up there?*

Chad laughed and gave Lester a lighthearted punch on the shoulder. *He's in an airplane, doofus, a rocket plane that can go faster than any other airplane in the world. He's going faster even than sound!*

Lester was confused and angry. Something big and important had happened and he was the only one in the world too dumb to know what it was. Paul kept looking at him and winking.

That night in their room Chad explained it to him over and over again until Lester at least learned to recognize terms like *shockwave, sound barrier,* and *Mach numbers.* Chad filled their room with plastic models of every plane in the Air Force, from big four-engine B-51 bombers to sleek new jet fighters. He hung them with transparent fishing line from the ceiling and displayed them on his desk with open canopies revealing perfectly painted cockpits all the way down to the tiny flight instruments and ejector seats. He built a red radio-controlled biplane one summer. He took Lester to a clear spot in the scrub behind their housing development and Lester watched as Chad started the little coughing propeller and then flew it into the sky. He marveled when Chad made it climb, dive, turn, loop-the-loop, and barrel roll, then landed it perfectly back where it had started when the engine ran out of gas and sputtered.

As he got older Lester came to love airplanes, but not like his brother. He loved them in a hand-me-down sort of way. He loved them partly because Chad loved them and partly as things that might hold the place in his soul that otherwise would have been empty.

Lester was fourteen when Chad went off college. In his first semester at State Chad joined Air Force ROTC. He called home and told his parents he was going to learn to fly, and Willy bragged all over town about his boy who was going to be flying fighter jets for Uncle Sam in a few years. Four years later, Chad was as good as his word. They sent him to Colorado Springs for flight training, first in little propeller planes that he joked could hardly stay in the sky. Soon he transitioned to a jet trainer called the T-33 Shooting Star which was almost but not quite a real live jet fighter. Chad called Lester every couple of weeks from Colorado to tell him of new adventures, new maneuvers he'd learned, new limits that he'd pushed and broken. As in college, he was at the top of his flight training class and when he graduated he told Lester they were giving him his pick of assignments. Any plane, anyplace in the world.

Back in Riverside Lester graduated high school, barely.

Chad received his wings a week after Lester's nineteenth birthday. The Air Force gave Lieutenant Morris a week's leave to visit home before he shipped off to Germany.

That's where the action is, Rusty, Chad said conspiratorially after dinner on his last night at home. Mom made Chad's favorite meatloaf and Lester watched enviously as his big brother shared a beer with their dad just like a grown-up. The brothers sat in the backyard under the half-sky of stars. Chad said, *See, Rusty, we've got a base over there, and it's less than nine minutes flying time from East Germany. The Reds have their own base about fifteen minutes from ours, too. So if anything happens, Rusty, your big brother's going to be the first one in the scrap.*

Lester thought of his brother strapping into his gleaming fighter, snapping a salute to his ground crew and then roaring skyward in a blaze of afterburners and acrid jet exhaust. And then he thought of his own daydreams, the ones that didn't visit him much these days, and he remembered the white line in the sky.

He asked, almost embarrassedly, *Have you ever seen your own contrail?*

Chad laughed and slapped his brother's shoulder. *Seen it? I've flown right through it! That's how you know when you've done a perfect maneuver, like a loop, when you fly right back through your own contrail.*

A plane passed overhead with blinking lights and a distant whisper of engines in the night that reverberated off the mountains and then faded away. Chad fell into deep thought. He said, *You know, Rusty, I love that sound. I love that sound more than any other in the world, even more than the sound of a girl laughing. I love the sound and the sight of them, and the smell, the smell of jet fuel. It's almost better than the smell of pussy!* Chad paused, winked at his little brother, and repeated, *Almost.*

Lester laughed along with his brother, hoping he came across as casual enough. Chad grew serious again. *You need to find something like that, Rusty. Find something you love more than anything in the world, and go do it. You've always been good at stuff. You're twice as bright as most of the guys in my unit, and I'm saying that man to man, not as your brother. Don't waste your time in this town. Dad and Mom aren't going to be around forever, and if you just live your life the way we used to when we were kids, well.*

Lester heard the tone of despair in his big brother's encouragement. It was as if Chad knew, deep down, what Lester knew about himself: he wasn't smarter than those other pilots and that, in fact, he wasn't good at much of anything. Lester often wondered what he loved and what he might be good at, but his thoughts always traced back to that white line in the sky, and the dreams he knew would never come to pass even when they were still only dreams.

As it turned out, Chad never made it to Germany. Two days before he was scheduled to ship out he was on a training mission in an F-104B Starfighter. It was the Air Force's newest, fastest, and most dangerous interceptor. It was essentially a huge turbine engine with tiny wings built to fly at speeds and altitudes that the men who designed it still barely understood. It turned out to be nearly as dangerous to its pilots as to its enemies. Something went terribly wrong and Chad's plane went into a spin at somewhere near the speed of sound. His jet was cruising straight and level at 44,000 feet, the lead plane in a four ship flight heading out to the Carson Air Force Weapons Range in Colorado. He led them into a gentle, descending bank to the east, when his left aileron locked up and sent his plane cartwheeling out of the formation like a falling star slipping out of a constellation. At the inquest the radar operator testified that he watched the blip from Chad's plane drift across his screen, senseless in the black electronic oblivion that surrounded it, the transponder indicating a crushing loss of altitude. Chad must have fought the spin, because it wasn't until he was barely 2,000 feet over the ground that he ejected. It was too late. His parachute didn't open all the way and his body slammed into the alabaster desert floor a half-mile from his plane's smoldering crater.

When the rescue team arrived in their giant orange-and-white helicopter the smoke from the wreckage and Chad's canescent parachute undulated together in the downdraft like some lurid choreography. They picked him up and rushed him to the base's hospital but there was little they could do. His body would linger for a few days but everyone knew Chad was gone.

The family got the call that afternoon, and the next morning the Air Force flew the family to Colorado. Lester had never been on an airplane before, and as the massive four-engine silver transport rumbled up the tarmac a sense of panic gripped his guts. He started to say something to his father, but Willy was staring over the airfield as though something on the runway, or perhaps up in the mountains, held the key to Chad's life. Lester may as well have been invisible. His parents hardly spoke to him on the flight and by the time they landed in Colorado Springs he felt like a trespasser, an interloper who didn't have any business sharing their grief.

Chad, who Lester had come to believe was invincible, lay in a hospital bed with his bloodied face contorted into a expression of surprise. He was hooked up to a dozen beeping life-support machines and a respirator kept him breathing. The sounds of medical devices made the hospital room feel otherwordly, like a place out of one of the science fiction comics that Lester and Chad used to read with a flashlight under Chad's covers. Lester stood there dumbly, lost in the unreality of it all. A doctor who looked barely older than Chad himself stepped into the room and hooked up a new machine, explaining, *This is to help your son maintain his kidney functions. If his kidneys aren't working properly then the urea could build up and poison his blood.*

Willy said quietly, *Piss blood.*

Gladys said, *William!* She choked back a sob.

The doctor replied, *Not exactly, Mr. Morris. If the kidneys shut down the waste that becomes urine builds up in the bloodstream.*

Willy repeated, *Piss blood.*

Lester wanted to punch the doctor in the face. Who was he to say what was going to happen to Chad? Who was he to talk to Pop and Mom as if they were children themselves and not the parents of the best fighter pilot in the US Air Force? He pressed himself into a shadow in the corner of the hospital room and watched his brother. It seemed like his brother's every function was being supported or performed by a machine, the wires and tubes snaking about the room as though the Air Force was seeking to make up for its sin against his brother by throwing every piece of modern medical heroism at him they could find.

On the second night Lester managed to have a conversation with his brother. Pop and Mom had gone to the hotel to try to get some sleep. In the fluorescent, septic nightmare of the military hospital room Lester pulled a chair next to the bed and held Chad's limp, bruised hand. To his shame, he wept.

In a voice that seemed to originate from somewhere far from his brother's mouth, Chad whispered *Things didn't work out the way we planned, did they, Rusty?*

Lester choked back tears. *Don't say that, Chad. You're gonna be fine. Why, you're looking better every second to me!*

Lester thought he saw his brother smile. *Shit, Rusty, you're a worse liar than Pop.* He paused, comporting his strength. He took a rattling breath and said, *I don't know what happened, Rus. The plane was fine. It was brand-new. Something locked up, something went wrong, I couldn't—it wouldn't—*

Chad's breath failed and Lester was seized with panic. Finally, Chad gasped. He took a few more tortured breaths. *I didn't do anything wrong. You gotta believe me. You gotta tell Dad and Mom, tell everyone, I didn't do a goddamned thing wrong.*

Chad, no one thinks you did. You're the best pilot in the Air Force.

Lester felt the tears streaming down his face again and there wasn't anything he could do about them. Just like there wasn't anything he could do about Chad, or anything he could do about his own life. He suddenly was deeply jealous of his brother. He was going to die, but Lester was going to spend the rest of his life just like he'd spent the first nineteen years of it: stumbling along, sometimes looking up to see a white line across the sky and returning for a few minutes to a useless old dream.

Chad's voice was weaker by the moment, and Lester had to lean close to his brother's mangled face to hear him. *Rusty, I want you to make me a promise.*

Lester said, *Yeah, Chad, anything you say.*

Chad's response petrified Lester. *You gotta get your wings. There's nothing like it, Rusty. Nothing…like…it…in the world.*

Lester said, *I promise Chad. I promise.*

Chad took a shuddering breath and gazed into the lights above him. He spoke no more, though for another hour he blinked and even smiled once or twice. He stopped breathing near daybreak. Lester was asleep when his brother died. Chad, who loved airplanes enough to muster the courage to fly them near the edge of sound and space, whose very soul reverberated at the sound of turbine engines, who inhaled great lungs of jet fuel the way most men breathe a woman's perfume, was gone.

His parents had just arrived from the hotel when Lester stumbled into the fluorescent hallway and broke the news. Lester's failure was complete when he became the messenger of Chad's death. The failure that began as a little boy who couldn't even bring himself to play marbles or stickball with other kids accelerated like the white lines that appeared over his house. As though he bore responsibility as the vessel that delivered the news, the truant who skulked into the house long after midnight to whisper a nightmare come true: *Chad's dead and I'm alive. We all have to live with that.*

He didn't tell his parents how the nightmare ended, though. He kept his brother's last words to himself, the last secret he and his brother shared. But grief has a way of masking truth, at least at first. In the weeks and months after his brother's death the truth started coming back. It whispered to him at first but soon it was shouting. *You can't keep your promise to your brother. You can't do what Chad did. You'll never get your wings. You're going to let your brother down. You know it. You've always known it. You don't even have the guts to get a job.*

Chad's ghost lingered everywhere in Riverside Circle, so one day Lester decided to leave his hometown and move to Los Angeles. His parents, particularly Dad, had all but stopped speaking to him, anyway. He figured a city like Los Angeles was big enough that he could lose himself there, and hide from any memories that may chance to follow him.

Lester didn't get his wings but he did get his private pilot's license. In LA he discovered ghosts don't need familiar environs to do their haunting. They followed him to Los Angeles, to the small efficiency apartment he rented in Culver City, where he lay in bed at night listening to sirens, lunatic hobos, and the occasional gunshot. They finally followed him to Santa Monica Airport, where he forced himself to take flying lessons. He paid for them by getting a job driving one of the gas trucks that zipped around fueling the airport's growing population of light planes.

He wasn't much of a student, not that that surprised him. It took him almost six months just to solo and nearly another year after that before he got up the courage to take his check ride. But he slowly built hours in Cessna Skyhawks and Piper Comanches. It got so that he felt more comfortable alone in the sky than anywhere else. He didn't exactly gain a reputation at the airport, but was known as That Guy Who Drives The Truck, Flies Every Chance He Gets, And Never Talks To Anyone. It was the closest thing to an identity as he'd ever had.

Lester was shocked when one day Neal Holland, who owned a banner-towing company based at the airport, offered him a job. It turned out to be the perfect job for a man like Lester Morris: he flew every other day and spent hours towing advertising banners across the Los Angeles sky. Alone. Most of the time he flew from Malibu to Huntington Beach, a ten-minute transit that required little of him but keeping the plane in the sky and watching for birds, helicopters, and other banner planes. He was paid to be by himself in the sky, almost as far from other human beings as he could get. He grew to love the job. In a way he'd found his place in the world.

One day in the summer of 1972 he was in one of the company's Cessna 185s above Venice Beach. It was a hot and smoggy day and the beach was packed. He was towing a big blue banner advertising

LA Dodgers tickets. He'd just made his turn to head back north to the airport to refuel when the engine started missing. He thinned the mixture to try and even it out but a few seconds later the engine died altogether.

He released the banner to extend his glide, but even then he had barely thirty seconds and nowhere to land. His only option was to ditch the plane in the ocean. Which is when it occurred to him: he could end everything right then and there. He could radio Mayday, and then dive his plane into the water and that would be that.

He toggled his mic. *Mayday, Mayday, Mayday, Cessna two-zero-four-four Sierra declaring an emergency. Five miles northwest of Santa Monica Airport over Venice Beach. One soul on board. Intend an emergency water landing, over.*

The water was racing toward him. He thought of Chad, he thought of the white lines in the sky that day in the backyard.

At the last possible moment he glanced toward the beach. People were racing toward the water, and he saw several men tear off their shirts and dive into the water. To save him.

The sight changed something inside him. He brought his wings level and dropped his flaps. He didn't want to die. He wanted to fly, every day for the rest of his life.

As he closed his eyes he thought, *What do you know about that, Chad? I did it right after all.*

The Ballad of Kandy Kim, Part 2

We mentioned that Kandy Kim's first pilot was a WASP from Tacoma, Washington, named Nora Hall. She'd just turned thirty-one and had been a WASP pilot for eight months, with nearly 500 hours logged in that short span. She was a serious, by-the-numbers kind of pilot but she also had an uncanny seat-of-her-pants instinct for airplanes that would have made her an ace combat pilot in a different world. Flight instructors tell their novice students to learn to *think ahead of the airplane,* the idea being a pilot who relies on reflexes at 10,000 feet and 300 miles per hour won't last very long. It becomes second nature to a good pilot, the way a concert pianist doesn't consciously think about the notes she's playing because her mind is several measures ahead and making split-second decisions about tempo, timbre, tone, and the like. The instinct usually requires intense training and dedicated practice since for most would-be aviators the cockpit is overwhelming even on the ground with the engine off.

Nora was different. The first time she slid into the rear seat of the creaky old Piper Cub in which she took her flying lessons she felt like she was settling into her favorite reading chair at home. She astonished her instructor, a World War I veteran with a swollen and discolored purple scar like a tangerine on his right cheek and a pronounced limp on the same side he claimed were given to him by the Red Baron himself. In eighteen months of combat and twenty years of flight instruction Jim Trick thought he'd seen everything. The notion had left him increasingly despondent. Pilots, for all their memorized checklists and procedures and protocols, are at their core adventurers. They are, in fact, quite like artists in temperament and outlook. Like an aspiring artist the would-be pilot wakes up each day with the vague sense that the world as she sees it, or as it is, is lacking in some essential way. In the artist the result is a spiritual or existential crisis: *I do not think the way the average man thinks, so I must find a new way of thinking.* For the pilot it is a physical crisis: *I do not see the world the way the average man sees the world, so I must find a new way of seeing.* The artist's reflex is inward-looking while the pilot's is outward-looking.

Perhaps both kinds of people are best thought of as seekers.

Nora's quest was amplified by other facts of her life. At an age when her school friends were working on their second, third, or fourth child Nora was not even married. She had lived with her roommate and companion Gladys Stotch for ten years. Gladys had been her closest friend since the tenth grade. It was the most fulfilling relationship she'd ever had, so much so that neither of them paid much heed to the whispers. Before the war Nora had been a teacher at Tacoma High School and a graduate education student at the University of Washington. A Wyoming ranch girl at heart, she found it inconceivable that school curricula required girls to sit at their desks for hours at a stretch repeating lessons like trained parrots. She was even more scandalized to discover that city girls knew less about their own bodies at seventeen or eighteen than she'd learned before she was old enough to saddle her own horse. It was downright ludicrous that girls should be taught how to keep a house and manage a family budget but not to keep or manage their own bodies. So she'd started a physical education program. When no one objected she started teaching girls' health, too. It never occured to her to ask for permission from her principal or the school board, she just started because she knew it was the right thing to do.

Along with twenty minutes a day of calisthenics, tumbling, jumping jacks, and the like, she held special weekly sessions in which she taught the girls about—well, being girls. At first she kept the sessions secret, required the girls to get their parents' permission, and swore everyone involved to secrecy. To her surprise a group of parents went to Principal McElroy and demanded the class be made part of the regular curriculum. There was a mild dustup with some of the more traditional-minded parents and school board members, but when no less than the University of Washington's Teaching Department weighed in on Nora's side the contentiousness died down. When she graduated three years later from the U with a master's degree in education, they ceased altogether. She still received the occasional dagger eye at the Piggly

Wiggly and from time to time a threatening missive appeared in the mailbox (usually postmarked from somewhere other than Tacoma), but the battle was over.

Nora emerged from the fight with a new sense of confidence in the parts of herself that she knew were different. It gave her the confidence to say, *I do not see the world the way other people see it, so I must keep finding new ways to see it.* Two weeks after she got her diploma an aviation booster came to town in a Curtis Buster. As the little craft of wood, canvas, and wires whisked her aloft for the first time, Nora wondered whether there might be something to that divine intervention stuff, after all. Still, Nora was above all a sensible person and she attributed the feeling to the combination of adrenaline, nerves, and the euphoria of flying into the sky the first time. Nora was also a confirmed atheist.

That is, Nora Hall was a confirmed atheist until the climb out from Everett Field near Seattle where she and her flight of eight Lightnings had stopped for fuel and lunch. Officially her plane was Lockheed P-38D No. 1138-926-8-42 and her call sign was Skipjack 3. Unofficially No. '8-42 was already Kandy Kim. Nothing in the four-hour flight from Palmdale to Everett on that autumn morning suggested Nora's plane was anything but P-38D No. '8-42. Nora had logged 140 hours in P-38s and she was head over heels in love with the futuristic airplane. It looked like two small airplanes connected by its tail empennage and wings. The pilot sat in a bulletproof egg-shaped capsule between the mighty 1,600hp Alison V-1710 turbo-supercharged engines. Visibility was exceptional thanks to the cockpit's forward location, the bubble canopy and the lack of a traditional fuselage. It was a virtuoso design that looked like it was going 400 mph sitting on the tarmac. And, oh, how that baby could fly! Advancing the twin throttles to even an inch produced a smooth roar of power that made the plane strain against its brakes (in fact the manual admonished fliers against applying the brakes at anything more than one-third throttle lest they tear apart). Push the throttles wide open and the plane screamed down the runway like a .50 caliber bullet.

Nora was lead in the second of two, four-ship echelons on the ferry flight to Alaska. The planes took off two at a time and the flight roared into a cloudless southern California sky. The flight commander, Major Nadine Pittman, had a well-deserved reputation as a hot shot. As soon as they cleared controlled airspace her voice crackled into the pilots' headsets. *Skipjack Flight, Skipjack One. Engines to military power and increase airspeed to three-five-zero knots on my call. Hee-readeee, go!*

Nora advanced the throttles and the acceleration pushed her into her seat. As the lead of her formation she kept her eyes on Skipjack 1, the horizon, her altimeter and her airspeed indicator. The planes in her formation would be watching her and spacing themselves accordingly. She accelerated smoothly and without affecting her altitude.

A few seconds later Nadine ordered, *Skipjack flight, climb and maintain one-seven thousand feet on my call. Hee-readeee, climb!*

The eight planes climbed in elegant symmetry. The regs called for ferry flights of P-38s to cruise at 280 knots and 10,000 feet. Major Pittman liked to fly high and fast, and she hadn't been rebuked yet. When they reached 20,000 feet she ordered the formations to space themselves widely. Formation flying was an unnecessary risk on a ferry flight.

In Everett the pilots debriefed the first leg of the flight over sandwiches and Coca-Colas. One of the WASP pilots' duties was to start each plane's squawk list, which would become one of the plane's official records. Squawks were pilot-speak for mechanical issues and they were particularly important to note on new airframes. Kinks and quirks discovered early could be fixed before they became problems. Nora was the only pilot without a single squawk. That was unusual in itself, and more so because Nora was a notorious splitter of hairs when it came to the planes she flew. It was where the seat-of-her-pants side of her piloting came out. She would squawk even things that *felt* wrong. With any other pilot—especially a WASP—such nit-picking would have driven the plane's new crews to distraction. Nora's reputation was such that the men who received planes she'd flown knew they were getting the opinion not just of a veteran pilot but an aviation savant.

Which may, when all is said and done, explain why Kandy Kim chose Nora. Or maybe it was that God, or the Fates, or whomever you chose to trust with your faith, arranged for them to meet. An exceptional airplane deserved an exceptional pilot.

Out of Everett Nora took off with Skipjack 7, her good friend Captain Dana Paul. They cleared the runway, raised their gear, and banked gently westward over Lake Washington. The sun floated across the surface of the lake, flashed like a strobe at its apex, and slipped back across the land. Mt. Rainer rose behind them from its forest bed.

Dana radioed, *It's so beautiful. I envy you for having grown up here.*

Nora keyed her mic to reply but at that moment her plane's throttles firewalled in her hand and she streaked away from her wingman. She pulled on the throttles with all her might but they stayed full forward as if bolted there. Her airspeed increased to 280kts, then 300, then 350. She was approaching 400 knots when suddenly the yoke pulled itself all the way into her stomach and the plane entered a vertical climb. Nora momentarily let go of the yoke and hauled on the throttle with both hands, to no avail. To her astonishment, in the next moment the rudder pedals kicked full right and the still-climbing plane half-pirouetted in the air, the yoke deflected the ailerons into a hard right turn and she was inverted. The controls reversed themselves and executed a flawless Victory Roll. She ended up in straight-and-level flight 500 feet above and a quarter-mile away from Dana. The throttles went forward again, and the yoke again was in her lap. This time she didn't fight but watched as the plane performed a beautiful loop. At the bottom it turned on its right wing, dived, and then came up and reassumed its formation with Dana.

The plane was hers to fly again. The maneuvers had lasted all of thirty seconds.

While descending in a bank to rejoin her wingman, Nora instinctively got on the radio. *Skipjack Three, Skipjack Three, Skipjack Three. Mayday Mayday Mayday. Declaring an emergency. Two miles northwest of the field over Lake Washington at five thousand feet. One soul on board.*

Everett Field Control responded instantly. A calm, professional male voice said, *Skipjack Three, Everett Control, acknowledge your Mayday. What is the nature of your emergency, over?*

Everett, Skipjack Three. Unintended departure from controlled flight. Which, as she spoke the words, Nora realized wasn't precisely the case. Her plane had departed from *her* control, that was for sure. The maneuver itself, however, was executed perfectly. Moreover, as she rejoined Dana her plane felt different. It was flying almost—demurely. Could that be right? She glanced over her right wing toward Dana, and the green position light blinked. Or at least, she thought it did. Like the plane was winking at her. That was the first time the words flashed through her mind: *Not just an airplane. Not just an airplane…*

She was entranced by the light (which now was the usual steady green) when her headset crackled again. Everett Control asked with militaristic calm, *Skipjack Three, Everett, state your intentions.*

Nora smiled under her oxygen mask. Intentions, eh, Control? Well, I intended to ferry a P-38D from Palmdale to Alaska. I intended to have dinner on base tonight, maybe get a little drunk, write a letter to Gladys then get a good night's sleep and catch a transport back to California tomorrow or Wednesday.

Oh, did you mean more generally? Well, I intended to serve out my duty until the war ends then settle back home to teaching and my life with Gladys. I intended to rekindle friendships, work through family problems, pay my taxes and bills, save for retirement, and half-heartedly go to All Saints Episcopal Church on Sundays because it's important to Gladys. I intended to take a two-week vacation every summer to places like the Grand Canyon and Yellowstone and Manhattan. I intended to read books to better myself, keep up on the news and world events, and volunteer once a week at the food bank. I intended to drink whiskey on my birthdays, cider at Christmas, and champagne on New Year's. I intended to get gray hair, grow old, and one day to die. Since even Gladys hasn't been able to persuade me about God, I intended my death to be a comfortable and complete darkness for which I intended to be quite prepared.

But, you see, Everett Control, that was before my airplane flew itself a loop and winked at me. That was before an invisible hand firewalled the throttles and pulled back on the yoke, before my airplane executed a more precise maneuver than I'd ever seen a human being pull off. And do you want to know the kookiest part? I wasn't scared. Not for a second, not one bit. In fact I felt as calm as I've ever felt in my life, calm enough to appreciate how beautiful the world looked as it spun and wheeled outside the canopy, calm enough to watch the sun flash across the face of Lake Washington and feel it warm on my face and think my goodness did God just caress my face?

I guess what I'm saying is that an awful lot has happened in the last couple of minutes and I'm still digesting it all—

Her headset crackled again. *Skipjack Three, Everett, say again your intentions. We've cleared the pattern for you and fire trucks are rolling toward the runway.*

Nora keyed her mic. *Ah, negative, Everett. Looks like it was just some surface flutter. I've got it back under control. Cancelling the Mayday call. Sorry for the trouble, over.*

Roger that, Skipjack Three, no trouble. Be safe up there, and we're here if you need us. Over.

Thank you, Everett. We're okay. Skipjack Three, out.

Roger that. Everett, out.

They crossed the Canadian border. Vancouver lay nestled against the hills off their right wings, and after that the land became wild, ten million acres of forest punctuated by snow-capped mountains and greenblue lakes and rivers.

On the plane-to-plane frequency Major Pittman said, *Skipjack Three, Skipjack Lead. Care to explain what that was all about, Lieutenant?*

Like I told control, Major, control flutter. I'm okay now.

That remains to be seen, Lieutenant. You just broke about a half-dozen regulations, and those are just the ones I can come up with off the top of my head. We'll be discussing this when we arrive. Meantime maintain altitude and airspeed. She added, as if talking to herself, *Good grief, even I wouldn't try a stunt like that.* Nora couldn't tell if her tone was exasperated or admiring.

Well, shit, Nora thought. Major Pittman's rebuke had made her feel like a little girl whose mother tells her they'll be discussing her behavior with father tonight. As they climbed between towering cumulonimbus clouds over the San Juan Islands she considered her answer. The more she rehearsed it the less she believed it. Her plane had departed controlled flight to flawlessly execute two demanding aerobatic maneuver seemingly of its own volition.

Wait—volition? An airplane was made of aluminum, steel, rubber, plastic, and glass. For all the talk among pilots about airplane's souls and personalities they never talked as though airplanes had consciousness, much less free will. This was the middle of the twentieth century in the middle of a war. Such head in the clouds musings could get you killed even if you weren't in a combat zone. Then again the alternative explanation was no more reassuring: maybe she was cracking up.

That night after supper, two stiff shots of whiskey and a surprisingly mild rebuke from Major Pittman, Nora wandered to the tarmac. It was after 2300 but the northwest sky glowed the color of lilacs, a thin line of pink at the edge of the mountains and the sea. The island was the color of a Denali forest at midnight, punctuated by the ghostly silhouettes of a half-dozen hangars, barracks, and the control tower. The base was blacked-out and the only artificial lights were occasional red or blue penlights bobbing vaporously between buildings as people went about the twenty-four-hour business of fighting a war. She walked toward the eight planes from Skipjack flight. They'd parked at a 45-degree angle in front of the main hangar. There were also a half-dozen B-17E Flying Fortress heavy bombers, an eighteen-plane squadron of big, single-engine P-40 Warhawk fighters, two Catalina flying boats for search-and-rescue, and two single-engine Piper Cub observation planes that looked like sparrows next to their enormous brethren.

Nora loved airports at night because they were full of secrets and stories. She always imagined the planes were whispering their adventures and talking of pilots, missions, scrapes and triumphs. Of course, before this afternoon she never believed they might actually be talking. Tonight, though, she hushed the imaginary conversations. She was listening for something real even though she couldn't for the life of her imagine what it might be. The only sounds were the hum of a diesel generator on the other end of the base, the whisper of waves on the island's rocky hide, and the occasional haunted call of a loon.

She stopped in front of Kandy Kim and let her eyes roam the sinuous, sensual metal lines. The butterflies fluttered in her stomach like they always did around airplanes and Gladys. Like every well-designed airplane since the Wright Flyer, Kandy Kim looked out of place on the ground. The P-38s landing gear were designed for rough and unfinished fields like the one the Seabees were building on South Pacific islands. They were masterpieces of engineering which, when extended on a 400 mph fighter plane, looked perfectly ridiculous. Nora felt the urge to take Kim into the sky, just *because.* She stepped forward to put her hand on Kim's left wing and realized her hand was shaking. Not in fear, but the way it shook the first time she'd touched Gladys's face. It was the feeling of finding herself on the edge of a great and wonderful discovery. She touched the leading edge outside the engine. The metal was warm.

She stepped back from the plane and folded her arms. *Well, then. You seemed to have something on your mind this morning. What was it you wanted to talk about, girl? It's just you and me out here now.* She half-expected a nav light to blink or an aileron to wiggle in greeting. Part of her hoped for something more, the part of her where love and piloting lived and where anything was possible. Even the possibility that an airplane could have a conscious. Even the possibility of God.

When nothing happened after a minute, she laughed out loud.

Okay, okay, I get it. You're operating on your own terms. For what it's worth I can relate.

Nora ducked under the wing and hoisted herself up next to the cockpit. Had it not been locked she would have settled into the seat one last time. Instead she unsnapped the buttons and pulled the canvas hood back. She cupped her hands and looked into the cockpit. The white-faced instruments were just visible, hanging ghostlike in the dark. Again she waited for something to happen, and again nothing did. She sat down on the wing with her back against the big engine nacelle. The night's first stars glittered on the southern horizon and the first dim outline of the Milky Way glowed like Kim's instruments overhead. A light breeze fanned across the tarmac and Nora shivered.

Jiminy Cricket! A five-knot breeze up here packs the punch of a gale-force wind back home. Doesn't bother you, though, does it?

It occurred to her that she'd never tried to have a conversation with an airplane before save for the occasional *'Atta girl!'* or coaxing through a particularly dicey crosswind landing. Now she was sitting on a fighter's wing trying to coax it into—what? The unease returned and she wondered all over again if she'd made up everything that happened earlier that day.

Hell with it, she thought, *it's not the first time I've raised some eyebrows.* She said, *I wish you could tell me how you got to be the way you are. I wish I knew how many there are like you. Unless you're one of a kind, and I hope you're not. You would be a pretty lonely gal. A gal like you deserves the right companionship. If I was a betting gal, though, I'd say the likes of Kandy Kim are few and far between.* She patted Kim's wing. *Well, take it from me. It might take ten years and ten broken hearts, it may require a pickaxe and headlamp, but one day you'll find her. Meantime, if you get lonely you just set your auto-nav for Tacoma Airport and I'll be waiting.*

The first notes of Taps drifted over the tarmac. *That's my cue, lights out.* She stood on the wing. *Thank you for an adventure I'll*

never forget, girl. I'll check on you once more in the morning before
I head home. Sleep tight.

Nora went to replace Kim's canopy cover when she saw a different glow from the instrument panel. The radio was on. Sure enough when she shined her penlight into the cockpit the radio and Nav/Com switches were both off. But there it was, the glowing radio. She heard something and pressed her ear against the glass. She heard distantly, a song she recognized:

> *I don't want to set the world on fire,*
> *I just want to start a flame in your heart.*
> *In my heart I have but one desire,*
> *And that one is you,*
> *No other will do…*

Nora swallowed a lump in her throat. It was one of her and Gladys' favorite songs. They had danced to it the night before she left for duty. Coming from the cockpit of one of the world's most powerful fighter planes, a machine designed to set as much of the world on fire as possible, it sounded like a plea.

She felt a tear roll down her cheek. It dripped onto Kim's wing. Nora caressed Kim's canopy and said, *You've got a different mission, don't you? Well, girl, I love you. I've never met anyone or anything like you. I'll be dreaming of you a lot, and like I said, if you ever get lonely you know where to find me.*

She took out a scrap of paper and her never-dry pen, and jotted a note:

> *Dear Pilot,*
>
> *This is Kandy Kim. She's not like any other airplane I've*

ever known. I have over 2,000 hours flight time in two dozen types of aircraft, and Kandy Kim is unique in every way. If I were to tell you why you wouldn't believe me. The other letter in the cockpit explains how she got her name, but I'm not sure I can explain Kim herself.

All I can say is this: if something happens, trust her. She'll take care of you. Take good care of her, too.

Keep the oily side down, flyboy.

Sincerely,

Lieutenant Nora Hall, US WASP Corps
September 13, 1944

She slipped the note under the canopy cover and jumped off the wing. She kissed the fighter's nose just below her pitot tube, leaving a small lipstick mark.

Dora's Adventure

Dora Hammond always loved traveling. One morning in mid-September she finished her breakfast and, looking out the window and seeing an airliner pass overhead, decided it was time for a new adventure. It was one of her favorite kinds of New York mornings, one that simultaneously felt like the end of summer and the start of autumn. She felt inspired. She went to the hall closet and pulled out a small leather satchel, perfect for a three-day excursion. A street sweeper rumbled by outside but she barely noticed her windows rattle.

After Harold passed away, her daughters and son had marveled at her independence. Well, not marveled, exactly. They knew their Mom was a strong-willed survivor. She assumed that what really surprised them was the fact that she was able to go on living at all, much less with vigor and energy. Dora Engh was nine days shy of her twentieth birthday when she ran off with a dashing lieutenant from Fort Ord named Harold Hammond. She was pregnant with

Caroline barely a month after the wedding in the little chapel in Las Vegas, which Harold would joke for the rest of his days was close enough for government work. Before a blood clot took him from her at the age of sixty-four they'd been married forty-two years. As far as her children could tell family was the only life she'd ever known.

She knew they wouldn't understand how, in a way, her decision to travel this morning was a tribute to Harold. The anniversary of his death was coming up. No matter what else was going on, this time of year focused her mind on the good times. The memories never went away but as the anniversary approached they came more frequently and rapidly. Their son Joshua, who had the unfortunate double distinction of being both the middle child and the only boy, said she sometimes seemed to just go away. Dora couldn't argue with Josh, who at twenty-nine was an introverted and deliberative accountant at a small firm in New Rochelle. He grew up wedged between his little sister Sabrina, who was the most beautiful girl in every room she ever walked into, and big sister Caroline, who from the moment she could put two words together acted liked she owned every room she walked into. Since Sabrina was less than two years his junior, the happy accident of the family, many of the boys who called themselves Josh's friends over the years hung out with him solely for the opportunity to see the inside of Sabrina Hammond's room or to have dinner at the same table as the Daffodil Queen. More than a few bras and panties went mysteriously missing over the years. Dora covered by saying the washing machine ate them. Sabrina didn't believe her mom's fib any more than Josh believed the boys who sat ogling his little sister at the dinner table were his friends, but these were the sorts of mundane mendacities upon which so much modern contentment rested.

As usual it was Harold who kept her from succumbing to her cynicism about the fate of the young generation generally, and her daughters in particular. One of the magical aspects of their marriage was the way they compensated for each other's bêtes noires or, as Harold called them, utterly irrational and completely justified paranoias. Where Dora was prone to seeing sex fiends in the making sitting at their table Harold saw teenage boys who were mostly harmless. Besides, Dora had a reputation as a no-nonsense kind of mother, and Harold was a marine with two turns in the war under his belt. No one was going to mess with their girls.

In bed the evening after a particularly infuriating episode— Dora had actually caught Rob "Ringer" Roman rifling Sabrina's underwear drawer while the kids were supposedly shooting baskets in the driveway—Harold told her that when he was fifteen he'd done the same thing to his best friend's big sister. From his side of the bed he gave her one of his sideways grins and teased, *Ahh, Bethany Miller. Dore, you should have seen her!* He comically cupped his big, work-calloused hands in the air above his chest. *I mean, dey was huge! And as it turned out she was a bit ahead of her time in the thong panty department.* He sighed in mock contentment. *Ah, memories.*

Dora playfully bopped him on the head and then wrapped herself around him. Panty raid or no panty raid Ringer was still one of the good ones, a goofy kid with braces like Amtrak rails and a laugh like a horse whinny. Harold made her see that again, which was one of the ten thousand reasons she loved him

It was also part of the reason, with the anniversary on the horizon, she was going to travel. Her world had felt increasingly dark in the last year and she could feel her old tendencies creeping back. For all the globetrotting she and Harold had done, and for all the trips she took on her own, lately her life increasingly consisted of her apartment and the four blocks around her midtown high-rise—she referred to it as the *filing cabinet* to the kids on days when the clouds descended and Harold was not there to lift them. Oh, the first few years she was in the building she'd gone exploring like her old self. She memorized the subway system and timetables (these she could still recall with near-digital accuracy) and took weekend adventures on the LIRR and Jersey Transit. Twice she even took the Capitol Corridor to Washington, DC. But her world had been shrinking and she knew it was the reason for her frame of mind.

At first, when the kids started to cool to her adventuring she took it in stride. She was getting older and she lived alone (a fact that made her prouder with each passing birthday and sadder with each passing anniversary). She was still sturdy but they worried about her taking a fall. And an older woman was easy prey for the less desirable elements who'd been reappearing in the city the last few years. In the lucid and methodical manner of children raised by a businessman and a schoolteacher they laid out their arguments and adduced their evidence. Lately though she started to feel their concerns were overwrought and fueled by the incessant crisis-mongering of the media age in which they'd grown up. She had given up trying to persuade Caroline and Josh to let her grandchildren out of their houses alone. Josh's wife Kaitlin even called Dora whenever there was an AMBER Alert, just to make sure she'd heard about it. It was only a matter of time before their media-manufactured fears alit on their widow mother who lived alone.

Whenever Harold saw her clouds gathering he would take her on an adventure, even if it was just a long weekend in New England or down on the shore. She looked at the wall calendar hanging next to the kitchen counter. It was September 14. The anniversary was in four days. She said to the air, *Well, Harry, I think it's time we go somewhere, don't you?* As she pulled the telephone book down from its shelf in the linen closet in the unit's entryway, she reflected that she could not even remember the last time she'd ventured off the island.

The uncertainty first hit when she hailed a taxi. The driver gave her a funny look when she told him her destination. She thought he was going to argue with her but then she slipped a fifty-dollar bill through the bullet-proof Plexiglas divider and said the same thing she always said to cabbies when she and Harold went to the airport: *That's for you, and there's another twenty in it if you'll get me there and I don't have to run for my plane.* After that he was friendly, and since he was young to boot she let it slide. Traveling put her in a gracious mood.

But he kept looking at her in the rearview mirror with that same look in his eyes. She was tempted to ask him what the matter was, but what if he was unstable? What if it wasn't something she had said or done but something in his mind was projecting onto the innocent woman in his cab? No, she decided, it was best not to say anything. Some sleeping dogs should be left to snore, as Harold would say.

Besides, as the cab took the offramp toward the airport she felt the familiar excitement building in her chest. My, but she'd forgotten how big the place was, and how many jets there were! But of course she always felt that way upon seeing an airport. Not just her home airport but any airport in the world gave her the same boundless feeling and the same sense of enormous wonder. She caught a whiff of kerosene and jet exhaust and her heart fluttered. *Adventure, Harold! You're with me even when you're not. Of course it's not quite the same, I know that. How could it be? Nothing has been the same since I heard the crash and walked (I* walked, *Harold, why didn't I run? Would it have made any difference if I'd run to you?) into the bathroom and found you. But it's adventure just the same and I can still feel you and talk to you and know you're with me. We'll be up in the air again soon.* The driver looked at her again. Had she been talking out loud, she wondered? Then she laughed at herself again. *You're just a little nervous, it's okay.* A jet roared over the freeway.

Dora started out of her daydream when the driver rapped on her window. She heard him through the glass like a voice underwater, *Here we are, Ma'am. United terminal.*

He still got the terminology wrong but at least he had delivered her to the right place. She checked her watch. Not even 6:30 yet. She'd have plenty of time to catch her plane. He'd earned the extra twenty in spite of his less-than-professional demeanor. He was young, though, and taking stock of him on the curb while he retrieved her bag from the trunk she heard Harold. *Boys and young men are like wild animals, meaning they're a hundred times more afraid of you than you are of them.*

She suppressed a giggle when she handed him the extra tip. Now she quoted Harold aloud, "For services rendered, I thank you." She did a little curtsy. Being at the airport made her giddy and goofy.

When she stepped through the double electric doors her head swam again with the scope of the place. It seemed a hundred times bigger than she remembered and for a moment she felt woozy. She reached toward the wall to steady herself and nearly tumbled over when the wall turned out to be a huge palm plant. A young man with dark hair in a trim gray suit and red tie dropped his own bag with a clatter and grabbed her arm just as she started to fall.

Wowza! he exclaimed, *Steady there, ma'am. I gotcha.*

He helped her to a row of seats and she sat down heavily.

You okay? Take some deep breaths. You nearly took a spill!

I guess I did, at that. Dora managed a weak smile. *Thank you, young man. You probably saved an old gal's hip.*

He grinned. *Right place, right time, as they say. Can I get you a bottle of water or something? You look a little flushed.*

Yes, I think that might help.

He returned a few minutes later with Fiji water and Schweppes Ginger Ale. Dora was feeling better and she sipped the soda gratefully. She smiled, this time feeling it full and good on her face. *Even in New York City, there are still gallant and chivalrous men.*

A quizzical look passed his face for a split second, and then he guffawed. *That's a good one! Mind if I use it?*

Dora wasn't sure what he meant, but he was already retrieving his suitcase. She noticed it had built-in wheels. *Wherever did you get that suitcase?*

This one? Hmm. Can't remember. It's a Swiss Army, though. Great bags!

His answer plunged Dora into a fresh bout of uncertainty. A Swiss Army suitcase? Was that some new expression? She said, *That's very clever. It must do more than just carry clothes.*

This time he laughed right away. *Ma'am, I'm sure glad I ran into you. You've given me the two best laughs I've had all week! I've gotta train to catch but you have a great day, and travel safely wherever you're off to. Bye-bye!*

She watched him as the double doors snick-snicked open and closed and people passed. She realized everyone's suitcases had wheels except hers. The realization made her feel incredibly lonely and incredibly old.

The PA system boomed, *United Flight four-two-one with service to St. Louis and Denver will begin boarding in five minutes.*

Once again the emptiness in her heart evaporated and the thrill of her pending adventure filled the vacuum. It would be so good to see her sister Joanne, who lived in St. Louis with her husband. She went to the ladies room to freshen up and straighten her hair. Invigorated by a quick pee and a splash of water on her face she looked at the new digital sign and found her flight. Gate 83, now boarding. The security line wasn't bad. Sure enough it was barely five minutes before she was at the head of the line. She waited dutifully (feeling once again like an old hand) until the gate agent called, *Next.*

She stepped forward and began to put her things on the little conveyor belt. In the back of her mind she thought how much bigger the machines were than she remembered. There were new ones, too. She watched a man step into a contraption that looked like an elevator car and put his hands in the air. Her jaw nearly dropped when the inside wall started spinning around him, once clockwise and once counterclockwise. Before she could reason it out the gate agent barked, *Uh, excuse me, ma'am.*

She glanced over her shoulder and started when she saw him standing right behind her. She straightened and faced him. *What is it, young man? I have a plane to catch. St. Louis, United Flight four-two-one, is boarding. Didn't you hear?*

He cocked his head to the side. He was even younger than the Samaritan at the door, with crew cut blond hair, skin the color of peanut butter and the lingering evidence of adolescence on his face. To Dora he didn't look old enough to drive much less handle security at a major international airport. He said, *Sure, I heard it, and you'll make your flight just fine. But you forgot to show me your ID and boarding pass.*

The gloaming of uncertainty seeped back into the fissures of her day. With a shaky hand Dora pulled her driver's license from her wallet and handed it to the man. *Here's my identification. My ticket is at the gate, as per usual.*

On the rare occasion in the future when Dora thought about this day she would remember those words with bitter shame: *my ticket is at the gate, as per usual.* There was a pause which to Dora felt like a thousand minutes before the man said, *Ma'am, wait here a moment, please.*

He walked over to a waist-high wood cubicle where two other gate agents sat. Only as he conferred with them Dora realized they weren't gate agents at all. Gate agents didn't wear government uniforms, they wore the uniform of their airline. These were—well, what were they? They couldn't be police, could they? The thought made her cold. She kneaded her hands together. What if they were police? Would they know? There had been that one other time—

The boy was standing in front of her, this time with a tall black woman who reminded Dora of the nice new Negro newscaster on Channel 7. A little broader in the chest and hips, maybe, and with long woven hair that would never pass muster at a network affiliate. But still, her face was pleasant and trustworthy, and she was smiling. Dora felt she was the one who would set the young man straight.

Good morning, Mrs. Hammond. How are you?

I'm fine, thank you, though I'm beginning to worry about catching my flight. United Flight four-two-one to St. Louis, you know. It's been boarding for a few minutes now.

Yes, I know, and we'll get you moving just as soon as we can.

She smiled again and Dora sighed with relief. *Thank you, Miss…?*

You can call me Kimberly, Mrs. Hammond.

In that case I insist you call me Dora.

Now this was how things were supposed to work at the airport. In any government operation, for that matter. You found the one person out of one hundred who could get the job done. You introduced yourself, you fixed the problem together, and the next time you went to the airport you brought him or her a box of cookies or a copy of a book you'd enjoyed and wanted to pass along. From that point forward you had someone who would look after you. Someone in your corner, as Harold would say. Dora began to feel this Kimberly was her new friend at the airport.

Dora it is. The problem we have, Dora, is that your driver's license is expired. It's actually really *expired. Now, I might be able to let you slide on that, but you definitely need to track down your boarding pass. Federal regulations do not allow me to let you into the boarding area without a boarding pass.*

Dora waved a hand. *Why, Kimberly, that's absurd! I've never needed a boarding pass in my life! The airline keeps them for us at the gate as a courtesy.*

She saw Kimberly exchange a look with the young man but Dora's faith in her new friend was unshaken. *I don't know how long it's been since you last traveled, but that's the law. Where's your boarding pass, Dora?*

Dora was getting exasperated but she couldn't show it. If you crossed your airport friend she could become your airport nemesis, and you didn't want one of those. An airport nemesis could result in lost luggage, missed connections, even cancelled reservations. No, she wanted Kimberly on her side. *I told you, it's at the gate. Can't you just call over there? A nice fellow by the name of Hank Kemp used to help me and Harold. Oh, goodness, please hurry! They've been boarding for ten minutes already!*

She knew Kimberly could hear the desperation in her voice but she didn't care. No security mix-up, or whatever this was, was going to keep her from visiting her sister in St. Louis. Kimberly said, *I'll radio to have someone ask at the gate. But I don't think you should get your hopes up. Things have been pretty tight around here since nine-eleven.*

Now Dora did lose her temper, albeit briefly. *Niney-what? Young lady, you are talking nonsense. Would you kindly let me go to my plane right this moment? This is getting rather ridiculous.*

For the first time Kimberly was brusque. She pointed at the badge on her breast pocket. *Mrs. Hammond, do you see that? I work for the Transportation Safety Administration. That means Safety is my middle name, and right now you're not safe. So you wait.* She added in a softer tone, *With me.*

Dora was stung by the rebuke. No, she was stunned by it, and the fact that she was Mrs. Hammond again and not Dora wasn't lost on her. What on earth was this security guard doing? It wasn't as if Dora Hammond looked like a criminal, much less a terrorist. What did she mean, You're not safe? Had the whole world gone crazy in the time it had taken to get to the airport?

Kimberly nodded to the young man and the line began moving. Everyone seemed to have a current driver's license and a boarding pass. She was vaguely amazed how docile the passengers were, considering the indignities to which they were being subjected. Well, if these people expected her to take off her shoes and take the pins out of her hair and God knew what else, on top of delaying her with this ridiculousness, they had another thing coming.

The PA announced other flights, and then Dora heard, *This is the final boarding call for United Flight four-two-one, service to St. Louis and Denver.* She tried to ask Kimberly another question but the words were a jumble in her mind. The line at the metal detectors had grown longer, snaking through a rope maze and starting a line down the terminal. The people in front weren't wearing the expressions of happy travelers. They looked, actually, downright hostile. They were looking at her and for the first time Dora was frightened. She felt that she was waking into a nightmare, face after face turning to her with the same disgusted scowl. She was grateful for Kimberly who seemed at least to be neutral in the situation.

Kimberly snapped, *What you doin'?*

Dora hadn't realized she'd clutched her friend's forearm, the one above her mace can and handcuffs. She let go like the arm was a thousand degrees. *I—I'm sorry. I'm just frightened.*

Kimberly patted the offending hand. She actually smiled. *You must be. You've had a busy morning. But don't worry, we'll get everything sorted out.*

The PA boomed again, seemingly louder, *Final boarding call for United Flight four-two-one with service to St. Louis and Denver. All passengers please make your way to the gate immediately. This is United four-two-one, final boarding call.*

Dora tried once more. *Kimberly, please. I'm going to be late and I can't miss my flight. My sister is expecting me. She isn't well.*

The last part was true, if an exaggeration. Joanne's cancer had been in remission for almost five years. Still, she was going to visit a sister with cancer and that ought to be enough to put a little fire in any security agent's pants. But Kimberly shook her head. *If it was up to me, Mrs. Hammond, you'd be sitting in First Class with a glass of champagne on your way to your sister's. But it's not up to me. It's up to them.*

She nodded at the two portraits on the far wall, one of the President and one of the Governor. Suddenly Dora's desperation was gone. She did not feel panic but the sort of release you felt when you accepted, finally, that you've missed your flight. She sat down and Kimberly, who really was quite sweet, patted her shoulder. *We'll get everything sorted out.*

They would. The airline would make everything right the way they always did. If there was one thing left in this country that still ran like clockwork it was the airlines, and especially United. Why, hadn't she and Harold received a personally-typed letter from the regional Vice President the time the airline lost her suitcase on the way home from Hawaii? Besides, there had to be more then one daily flight to St. Louis from New York City.

She watched contentedly as the throng of passengers processed through security. The mean faces were gone, already on their way to their airplanes, and she watched the sea of strangers. A final sort of calm descended upon her, the calm of anonymity. That was one of the things she loved about travel, being in places where no one knew or cared who you were. It was liberating and let you experiment with different parts of your persona. In foreign cities a shy office clerk could be a Lothario and the demure librarian could strut the beach in a string bikini.

Kimberly interrupted her musing. *Okay, Dora honey, here we go. These folks are from the Port Authority and they're going to help you out.*

She looked up to see two police officers, a tall man who looked barely older than the gate agent and a stout woman of perhaps forty with a crew cut and glasses. Both had pistols, mace, and handcuffs on their belts. Dora was astonished. She turned to Kimberly, her airport friend. *You called the police? What on earth? Have you all* lost your minds? *I'm just a woman trying to visit her dying sister in St. Louis!*

We'll get you to St. Louis just as soon as we clear up a couple of questions, Dora.

The female police officer reached for Dora. *Hello, Mrs. Hammond. Sorry to bother you, but if you'll come with us—*

Dora swatted her hand away. *Don't you touch me! I'm an American citizen and I have rights!* People were starting to look again but she didn't care. She had to get on that plane. She had to see Joanne, before it was too late. Oh, she would never forgive these busybody bureaucrats!

Ma'am, please, we don't want to—

Exasperated, Dora said, *This is all about a ticket, is it? Well, why didn't you just ask me for my ticket in the first place?* She looked at Kimberly. *Is that what this is about, my ticket?*

Kimberly looked at her helplessly. She spread her hands. People weren't just staring, several had left their precious places in line to watch the police harass a poor little old lady on her way to see her sister one last time. Well, she would show them.

It all made sense. She felt a sense of triumph. As Harold would say when confronted with a SNAFU that threatened to derail them, *There's always a seat on the plane.*

She unclasped her bag and held it out for them to see. She shouted, *Once and for all,* here's *my ticket!*

But her bag was empty. She stared at it and the world seemed to grow quiet, except that the female police officer said something into her shoulder-mounted walkie-talkie. Dora felt herself bordering on hysterical but she couldn't help it. Poor Joanne, already so frail, would be waiting at the airport in Kansas City and when Dora didn't arrive she would fly into a panic. That was the way Joanne had always been but these days such emotional shocks could be fatal.

Then she realized what had happened. The smirking, beady-eyed cab driver! She looked desperately at the two police officers. *The cab driver! He stole my things! He stole my ticket!*

The female police officer said gently, *Mrs. Hammond, your daughter Christine is coming to pick you up. A lot of people have been very worried about you since you wandered off last night. Why don't you come with us and we'll have a cup of coffee and you can give us a statement while we wait for her.*

Dora was defeated. Her grand adventure was a disaster. Christine would be beside herself for having to leave work and drive to the airport. She made one last small gesture. *May I use the telephone? I'd like to call my sister to tell her I'm not going to make it to St. Louis today.*

The police officers exchanged a look. The fellow pulled a cell phone out of his pocket. The woman said, *Charlie—*

I know, I know. But what's she going to do, call her al Queda contact in Afghanistan? Besides, we're right here.

Dora took the little phone gratefully. She was still not great with these things but she managed to dial Joanne's number from memory. It rang several times (Joanne was moving even slower than Dora these days), then her sister finally picked up. Dora started to say she was sorry, that there was a situation at the airport, when a strange voice told her, *The number you have reached has been disconnected or is no longer in service. Please check the number and dial again. This is a recording.* It repeated two more times before Dora hung up.

She gave the phone back to the young officer. She said, *She's gone, isn't she?*

The female officer nodded. *Yes. Your daughter told us. Your sister died twelve years ago, Mrs. Hammond. I'm so sorry.*

Kimberly, her airport friend, put a hand on her shoulder. Dora nodded. In her mind she saw a flicker of light as through a cracked door. She saw Joanne, and she saw the funeral. She saw Harold, too, and her own parents and her dog Maggie, the goofy chocolate lab whose only talent was being an absolute love. She saw things the way they had once been and never would be again. A wave of sadness crashed over her and for a half second she felt like screaming.

Then the door closed. Her memory spared her.

She looked back at the officers and smiled. *Just you wait until my Christine gets here. She'll straighten this whole mess out. Everyone's going to have some explaining to do.*

Water Bombers

At first it looked like a thunderhead, an anvil-shaped cloud developing over the mountains. The weather had been predicting heavy rain all week. Today it was a 70 percent chance. On Tuesday it was a 50 percent chance; on Monday, 30 percent. As though the weather service could will a thunderstorm from the drought by adding 10 percent to their predictions until nature gave in.

When they saw the gray filling the sky Darla figured maybe the forecast finally was right. She said, *It looks like we're going to get some rain.*

Tommy said, *Looks like a brush fire to me. Big one, too.*

He sipped his beer and watched the slow-moving wall. This was their outside time. Every evening at sunset they sat on the little balcony and watched the day disappear behind the big retirement building across the street. The mountains rose above it in the distance, and the cloud slowly obscured them. Darla and Tommy used to make fun of the old people hobbling in and out of the big tower.

Darla said, *The weatherman's been predicting rain all week. Thunderstorms. That would be nice for a change.*

Tommy burped. *If those are thunderclouds I'm a flying monkey.*

He'd gained weight since the surgery, his athletic frame adding its first surplus pounds. He looked older. She tried to see through the soft new layer and see the high school quarterback she'd married. He'd be thirty-nine in a month. She knew age eventually would catch up even with Tommy Zottner. It was the suddenness that surprised her.

He took a long breath through his nose and exhaled. *Do you smell that?*

Smell what?

Take a deep breath, you'll smell it.

She sniffed the air, and tried a long inhalation. She smelled the oil from the street, dry pungent oak leaves, a vague hint of dog shit from the sidewalk.

Nothing out of the ordinary.

Try.

It would help if I knew what I was trying to smell.

Do I have to give you all the answers?

He crushed the empty can and tossed it in the big orange Home Depot bucket that served as a trash can.

He heaved up from his beach chair. The surgery made it so he stood with his left leg comically straight. Sometimes when he walked he looked like a mime walking against invisible wind. An oversize, flannel-shirted mime.

Get you another, he said. It wasn't so much a question as a statement of intent.

Actually I think I'll switch. Stoli rocks.

The sun's still up, you know.

Thought you were tired of having all the answers.

He let that one hang and gimped through the living room to the galley kitchen. On the cracked sidewalk across the street Darla saw Pee-wee, the stray black and orange tortie the retirement tower's residents had semi-adopted. He rubbed along the cement wall until he found an old man's leg to wrap himself around. She took another sip and smiled at the cat.

She called over her shoulder, *Pee-wee's here.*

Tell him hi for me, Tommy said from the kitchen.

He came back out with two beers and a rocks glass with two ice cubes filled a half-inch from the top and garnished with a lemon wedge. She took the drink and held his cans of Coors while he engaged the intricate mechanics of sitting. Then she gave him the beers and he cracked one.

The vodka went down cold and exploded hot in her stomach. It felt good.

Tommy said, *Okay, you've got to be able to smell it now?*

No.

You just swigged vodka. That screws up your sense of smell. Give it a minute.

She sipped. *I can smell just fine. I smell smog, eucalyptus, dog shit, and you.*

You can't smell worth a damn, because if you could you'd smell sage smoke. Can't miss it. We'd have fires up in the canyon when I was a kid. I'd know it anywhere. You'll smell it. Just don't drink for a minute.

I'm not drinking, I'm having a drink. And I'd like to meet this doctor who told you vodka messes your sense of smell.

Wasn't a doctor, it's something everyone knows.

Apparently not everyone.

Just give it a minute. Humor me.

She set her glass on the little red plastic table next to his leg. He was wearing sweatpants even though it was still 90 degrees. The scar ran up his inner thigh from just above his knee to above his groin. He wore long pants because every time he saw it he wanted to put his fist through a window. Darla knew this because he'd done it twice.

Tommy opened his second beer. He didn't take his eyes of the gray sky. She followed his gaze. In ten minutes he'd go inside and resume his latest Netflix binge. She would sit out here with a book and her iPod and wait for him to fall asleep before having a cry. She'd give herself a few minutes to feel the emptiness and then she'd finish her drink and go inside.

Ten more minutes until he'd heave himself up and limp back into the living room. Even on such a beautiful evening. The sunset was beginning to color the sky.

She said, *Maybe we should barbeque. It's been a while since we've done that. I can run to the store and get a couple steaks and a few more beers.*

Probably up along ridge. Idiots walk up there smoking cigarettes or weed and don't think twice about pitching a butt into the brush. Maybe some other night. Do you smell it yet?

I'm supposed to smell sage, right?

Sage smoke. Like how the kitchen smelled the night I burned that chicken.

God, that was funny.

It was funny after *the Fire Department left, you mean.*

I don't know, that part was pretty funny, too. You offered the lieutenant a drumstick for his trouble.

It was the least I could do. Though if I'd known they were going to send us a twelve-hundred-dollar bill I would've shoved the whole damn chicken up his ass.

Tommy—

I'm just saying, we pay taxes so we can have a fucking fire department, and that fire department sends two engines and a motherfucking hook-and-ladder to a smoke detector. It's all the public union bullshit, and they have the fucking audacity to send me a bill for it.

Forget it.

Sure, forget it. You forget it. You're not the one who had to pay the fucking bill.

I offered.

Yes, you did, and it was very sweet of you. But I wasn't about to make you pay for my idiot mistake. But yes, it was very sweet of you. Just the principle of the thing drives me fuck-all nuts. But seriously, now, can you smell anything?

Tommy Z., so help me I will throw the rest of this drink in your face.

Not much of a threat, there.

Her glass was nearly drained. There was a vague rumble from sky. *It sounded like thunder,* thought Darla. It would be nice for him to be wrong. He needed to be wrong. After three months he'd forgotten how to risk even that.

She stood to refill her drink. *Get you another?*

Make it two.

Now who's drinking?

Just trying to keep up. Besides, I need to dull the pain. He winked.

So do I.

Is that so? Good to know how much it hurts you.

I didn't mean that and you know it.

Sure, I know it. Remember, I have all the answers. He turned and looked down at the street. *Looks like Pee-wee's angling for some old folks' chicken.*

You just have to be like that, don't you?

Like what?

Like that.

The same way I've always been?

You know, Tommy, that's what worries me.

She let that one hang this time and went to the kitchen. She put four ice cubes and cut the Stoli with some water. A little extra lemon juice. She took three beers from the fridge.

The thunder grew louder, and it echoed off retirement tower. Only it didn't rumble and recede the way thunder did. It was also coming from the wrong direction. It sounded as though it came from the west, not the hills where the gray wall was still growing.

Tommy said, *All right, how about a friendly wager?*

Sure, I like winning bets.

Take it easy. I'm trying to right the ship here.

All right.

A wager.

What kind of wager?

I'll bet you a beer that's a brush fire.

A beer?

Sure. If I'm right, you have to walk to the store and get me a beer of my choice. If I'm wrong, I get yours.

You'll walk to the store?

Why not?

A large plane flew low overhead. It was bright orange and red with two wing-mounted radial engines that bellowed like an old World War II bomber.

Tommy said, *And there we have it. That's a Catalina, an old warbird they've converted into a water bomber. Flying toward the fire.*

Are you okay?

Sure, I'm always okay.

Don't fool.

I'm not. I'm always okay.

It's been a while since you've been okay.

Makes two of us.

Well, aren't we a barrel of monkeys.

Flying monkeys, remember.

A second plane rumbled overhead. The same orange and red paint, the same pregnant bulge in its belly where it carried water. She watched it helplessly.

Tommy whistled between his teeth. *Whoo-ee. Must be a fast mover.*

Baby. I'm sorry. I'm sorry, baby.

No, it's okay. I like watching 'em. God, those are some beautiful old airplanes.

All airplanes are beautiful.

I don't know, there are some honkers out there. No one'd ever call a Super Guppy a beautiful airplane.

It does what it does perfectly. There's beauty in that.

Fair point.

I just know sometimes watching them—

I said I'm okay.

It's just with all the time you spend inside.

I said I'm okay, not that I'm interested in a discussion.

The planes flew in formation toward the gray in the sky. They banked gently to the north, seemingly in no hurry. There was a five-dollar bill sitting in her little jewelry box in the bedroom. The planes continued in their pattern.

They weren't flying towards the gray but turning away from it. They continued their lazy turn until they were heading up the coast. She watched them for a long time, until they disappeared, first the sound of their engines, then the planes themselves, and finally the faint trail of exhaust they left in the sky.

Tommy wasn't deterred. *Probably heading out to pick up more water. Means they already made a run. Must be a real big one goin' up there.*

Tommy—

Don't. Don't ruin it.

The airplanes—

Yeah, the airplanes.

I know what it does to you.

I said don't ruin it. I'm about to win a bet.

Darla watched the sky. At that moment there was a new rumble in the distance. This time it came from the gray. There was a flash of lightening, and a few seconds later another rumble.

Darla said, *If that's not thunder and lightning, then I'm the flying monkey.*

Wait.

What?

Damn it, just wait. Just—

There was a flash from the clouds, and a second rumble. The two planes reappeared, low against the mountains. A bright pink plume streaked the air behind the lead plane. It banked sharply away from the mountain. The second plane rolled in and repeated the first one's run a short distance downhill.

As it banked away another lightning bolt shot skyward, and the thunder swallowed the roar of the water bombers' engines.

Tommy shook his head. *I'll be damned. What are the chances?*

So who wins?

We both win, and we both lose.

Sounds about right.

He smiled and hefted himself out of his chair. *Guess I owe you a beer. Back in a flash.*

As he headed for the door, he planted a small kiss on her forehead the way he always did when he left the apartment. Except that he hadn't done it in two months.

Tommy.

Yeah.

How about getting some steaks while you're out.

You always have to push things, don't you?

The way I've always been.

Well, then. What the Hell. Steaks it is.

You know, Tommy, I always thought they were beautiful airplanes.

They were indeed.

Betty Pilgrim

*I learned to wander. I learned what every dreaming child needs to know—
that no horizon is so far that you cannot get above it, or beyond it. These
things I learned at once. But most things come harder.*

—Beryl Markham

I

Two hours into a flight from San Francisco to
Houston on a spring day in 2015 a Virgin America
Airbus A340-300 talked to Mary Lee Willits. She
was in a business class window seat reviewing
a summary judgment motion drafted by Larry
Bea, one of Drucker, Feldman & Schaeffer, LLP's less-than-stellar
young associates. Mary Lee detested wasting time, and reviewing
shoddy work was high on the list of things that did just that and
consequently pissed her off. She went through the draft with a red

felt-tip pen like an elementary school teacher. *Larry could use some schooling*, she thought as she circled another citation error. The red would be lost in the faxed version she'd send Larry this evening but covering his work in the color of blood gave Mary Lee a measure of contentment and made her feel like the hour wasn't a complete loss, billable or not.

Mary Lee couldn't crack the mystery of her dysfunctional relationship with time. By any reasonable estimation she'd spent hers exceedingly well. She grew up with two older brothers in a town north of San Francisco. Being the youngest and the only girl gave her an extra shot of competitiveness out the gate. In high school she was a Presidential Scholar and captain of the girls' volleyball team. Her prom pictures were in the town society pages. She was accepted at the Ivies but decided on Stanford to be closer to home, since forty years of Baby Boomer living had taken its toll on her parents, especially her dad. She was in the top of her class and after Stanford Law she joined a premier firm, worked for the most ambitious partners, and won most of her cases and nearly all her motions. Two years ago she became the firm's youngest partner. She brought in some big clients and paid cash for a million-dollar townhouse in SOMA with a view of the bay and a balcony just big enough for a barbeque.

One of the only black marks was a failed marriage, but even then she didn't waste time. She'd given Mike precisely one chance to explain the lipstick on his collar that wasn't hers. His eyes had dropped and he'd mumbled a half-baked (it was more like a quarter-baked) excuse about hugging a coworker. Her first phone call the next morning was to a law school classmate who specialized in family law. No agonizing, no couples therapy (in the Bay Area even half the stable couples she knew were in therapy), no sobbing over glasses of Pinot Noir with girlfriends. She gave Mike a week to clear out and went to stay with her parents. She'd been single for the three years since, with the exception of a deeply satisfying rebound with the contractor she hired, rather fittingly, to redo the bedroom to eliminate vestiges of what's-his-name. These days she lived alone but never felt lonely. It could be argued, as the Airbus crossed the New Mexico border, that she hadn't wasted so much as a minute of her thirty-eight years.

Yet when the flight attendants came by with the drink cart and she paused her evisceration of Larry's version of practicing law to order a ginger ale, she felt the dread sense of time slipping away. It came on like an unpleasant case of déjà vu, and it had been happening more often lately. She could be sitting in Dolores Park on a Sunday afternoon eating a food truck pupusa (her favorite) and it would hit her: she was losing time. It was a physical feeling akin to what some people might call an anxiety attack. She imagined it was like living with a chronic health condition your doctor said might but probably wouldn't kill you: deep down you knew you were okay but every now and again the worst case scenario kicked its way into your imagination and started knocking over furniture.

The flight attendant, a twenty-something guy with expensive hair and excellent skin, said, *Uh, Miss—your ginger ale.*

Mary Lee realized she'd been staring out the window while he poured her drink. She reached for it. *Sorry. Spacing out.*

His smile combined sarcasm, condescension, and politesse as only a hip young flight attendant on a hip young airline can. *It happens. I'd like to space out but I have to serve drinks.*

She almost replied, *Don't strain yourself, honey,* but held her tongue. Engaging a snarky flight attendant was an excellent way to waste time. She set the ginger ale on her tray and went back to work.

A half-hour later she needed a break from the grammar apocalypse. She slipped the motion into her carry-on and tapped the menu on her entertainment screen. Playing a game or watching TV for a few minutes wasn't wasting time. It was a brain break, and breaks were necessary. She scrolled the options on the touch screen and chose a game called Word Slam, in which you had two minutes to come up with as many words as possible out of ten letters. It was mental exercise, definitely not time-wasting.

While the game loaded she glanced around the cabin. Her seatmate, a man in his fifties whose pinstripe suit and slight paunch suggested he spent a lot of his time sitting in business class, was snoring lightly. Most everyone else was dozing, too. It was an 8:00 a.m. flight and people had boarded in the semi-conscious daze of morning travel. *What a waste of time,* thought Mary Lee, shaking her head. *You took the early flight so you could work in the air and still have part of the day left when you landed.*

The screen beeped. She popped the little remote control out of the center console and prepared to give her brain a little spin class when her hand stopped dead in mid-air. She would forever remember it as the first time in her life she quite literally did not believe her eyes. In orange letters the screen said: *Time's a-wastin', Mary Lee. Time's a-wastin'.*

The phrase blinked and changed colors. It flashed like an old-fashioned Las Vegas neon sign and the letters got bigger and smaller like the old Windows screensaver. Mary Lee shook her head and blinked. She rubbed them like a cartoon character. The phrase bounced across the screen.

It's a trick, she thought. *Or it's part of some hidden camera show and I'm supposed to lose my marbles before Donnie Osmond steps out of the lavatory with a microphone and everyone laughs.*

And yet... *Time's a-wastin', Mary Lee.* It was what she said to herself whenever she felt unproductive. She had no idea where she'd first heard the expression but she liked the country ring to it. It was a sort of mantra. And now it was flashing at her from an airplane video screen.

Mary Lee reached for the flight attendant button over her seat. As soon as she pushed it and heard the *ding* the message vanished. A moment later the Word Slam logo and mascot, a little orange creature that looked like a cross between Elmo and a sick ostrich, flickered across the screen.

Ginger Ale Boy appeared. *Yes?*

She realized asking him about the screen would be a waste of time. She said, *I'm sorry, I had a question but I managed to answer it.*

He sighed theatrically. *Of course you did.* He reached up and clicked the button. *Let us know if there's anything else we can do.* He flounced away.

The remainder of the flight was uneventful. Still, Mary Lee was on edge during her thirty-six hours in Houston. She was there to defend a client's deposition, a task most litigators found mundane but that she relished. She defended her clients' depos aggressively and strategically.

At least, she usually did. This time her mind kept wandering from the conference room. She stared over the Houston skyline like she'd stared out the airplane window. *Time's a-wasting, Mary Lee, Time's a-wasting.* She nearly missed key objections and by the end of the second day her client asked if she was feeling okay. She played it off, reassured him they'd made a good record. She left out the part about the talking screen.

II

IT HAPPENED AGAIN ON the return flight. This time she hadn't even activated her screen. Two hours into the flight she glanced up from the Third Circuit case she was reading. The letters were red and they repeated across the screen until it was full: *You have all the time in the world, Mary Lee, all the time in the world.*

For the first time, she felt something start to come loose. It was as if she'd been pedaling a bicycle up a hill when all of a sudden the chain slipped. It threw off not only her progress but her balance.

She pushed the flight attendant button. As before, the screen went blank. A woman roughly her age with a pleasant, plump face and a bob that would have been at home in a 1960s Pan-Am ad, strolled to her row. *What can I do for you?*

Mary Lee relaxed slightly beneath the woman's bright-as-the-sun-at-35,000-feet smile. She felt more than a bit silly when she asked, *I was just wondering whether the airline ever tests new programs on the entertainment screens. Mine seems to be acting funny, and it's the second time in as many flights.*

The attendant furrowed her perfectly-plucked eyebrows in a sort of mock consternation that Mary Lee figured had been good for a lot of cocktails from businessmen in airport bars over the years. *I haven't heard of anything like that. What happened?*

Mary Lee felt the slip again and suddenly realized what her answer—her real answer—would sound like. A fruitcake in an Armani, that's what. She demurred, *Oh, it acted funny when I was playing the word game—Word Slam. It kept giving me too many points and restarting.*

Mary Lee's lame excuse wouldn't have fooled a sixth-grader, but the attendant was in half-listening mode, her eyes flitting toward a crying baby in the main cabin. *Well at least it was a good glitch. To tell you the truth they're still working out a lot of kinks in the entertainment system. On a flight last month every screen got stuck on an old Barbara Streisand movie on loop for six hours and we couldn't turn off the main cabin sound. By the fourth time she sang "Memories" people were ready to jump out of the emergency exits.*

Mary Lee laughed as the attendant straightened up and prepared to beeline for the now-screaming infant. *I'll ask the head steward; maybe she has some information.* She clicked the orange button off.

Mary Lee waved a hand. *Oh, that's okay. I'm sure it's just a little software bug. Don't bother the steward. You guys have better things to do.*

Are you sure?

Yes. I think I'm going to take a nap, anyway. Thank you.

For the first time in her life Mary Lee slept the rest of the way through the flight.

She woke with a start. She'd slept through not only the flight but the landing and taxiing. In fact the plane was nearly empty, only a few stragglers with kids and an elderly Chinese couple still making their way to the door. She unbuckled her belt and started to stand when the screen blinked again. *You have all the time in the world, Mary Lee.*

She said out loud, *Well, which is it?*

The Chinese couple looked at her as they passed and she smiled embarrassedly. *Fruitcake in an Armani is right*, she thought.

She hurried through SFO's International Terminal where time was a tangible presence and everyone was at its mercy: arrival times, departure times, delays, connections, layovers, cancellations. People hustling to make final boarding calls before time cut them off. She passed a Beats headphone stand and heard a snippet of a Rolling Stones song, Mick Jagger crooning, *Tieee-aye-ee-ime, is on my side, yes it is…* The distressingly gorgeous poster models in the window of the Tag Heuer watch shop leered at her. Everywhere people were checking watches, looking at clocks, pulling out smartphones to check the time. The time, the time, the time, which was sending Mary Lee's world spinning into chaos.

She nearly burst through the terminal doors into the cold Frisco evening. Her ride, a black Uber SUV, was just pulling curbside and she got in without waiting for the surprised driver to open the door. As he accelerated up the viaduct toward the crowded Highway 101 he said, *Sorry I was a little late. We've had a busy evening with the convention and all. Time flies when you're having fun!*

Mary Lee winced. *Sometimes it does even when you're not.*

He laughed. *True that. Ever notice how everything they come up with to make life more convenient seems to just make everything move faster instead?*

Oh, great, a philosophical Uber driver. She settled back in her seat and took an exaggerated breath. *I'm just glad to be home and have a few minutes to relax.*

He got the hint. He turned on NPR. Terry Gross was interviewing the new *Cosmos* guy, Neil deGrasse Tyson. Dr. Tyson was saying, *Put simply, time dilation means the faster you travel through space the slower you travel through time. In nineteen seventy-one scientists put atomic clocks aboard two airliners, one traveling east, that is, with the earth's rotation, and one traveling west against it. They kept a third clock on the ground. The eastbound plane traveled through space faster than the one traveling west because it had a cosmic tailwind. Relative to the clock on the ground the east-traveling plane lost about fifty nanoseconds, while the plane traveling west gained about fifty nanoseconds. So even on an airliner you're experiencing the relativity of time, and we can prove it—*

Mary Lee nearly shouted, *Oh, come* on!

The driver looked at her in the rearview. *Sorry, traffic's lousy tonight.*

She didn't hear. She jammed her earbuds into her ears and listened to Pandora while she scrolled through the roughly seventy-five emails she'd received during her nap on the plane. She only half-read them because her mind was trying desperately to rationalize the mysterious messages. Maybe it *was* a joke, or maybe it was some airline employee's idea of an inspirational message, like the ones they insist on putting inside iced tea lids.

Of course! She smacked her forehead and nearly laughed out loud. The driver gave her another glance. These days it seemed every company thought the best way to connect with customers was through banalities from people like John Lennon and Joan Baez. *Time's a-wastin'* was just the sort of faux-folksy message a hip airline like Virgin America would trot out. As for her name, well, she was on the flight manifest, wasn't she? The second message was a little more abstract but it still made sense. Especially if the kid coming up with the inspirational phrases was a stoned college intern. As for the Stones song and the hundred clocks in the terminal, well, of course she'd noticed them more than normal.

As they slowed in South San Francisco traffic Mary Lee took out her earbuds. She liked Fresh Air, and *Cosmos* was in her Netflix queue. Terry was asking Dr. Tyson more about the relativity of time. The last thing she heard Dr. Tyson say was, *The more I learn about the cosmos the less convinced I am that some sort of benevolent force has anything to do with it at all.*

Damn right, Doc, thought Mary Lee as she dozed off.

III

IT HASN'T TURNED OUT to be quite so simple. Mary Lee has begun to feel she's slipping permanently, moving from one time into another without pause. She'd been resisting it but now she accepts it. She looks for signs but when she tries she sees nothing. It's as if whatever is happening to her is by necessity in the periphery. It doesn't want to be discovered. Yet for two months now she's gotten messages on every single flight she's taken. It's gotten so she nearly has a panic attack the night before getting on a plane. She's tried different airlines, different airports but nothing works. A United 767 out of Oakland told her, *It's true, time flies when you're having fun, Mary Lee. Are you having fun?* A Continental A350-200 from JFK to SFO said, *No time like the present, Mary Lee, no time like the present.*

At first they were clichés, but recently the messages have grown increasingly personal. An Alaska Airlines 737-400 asked, *Are billable hours really more valuable than free ones, Mary Lee?*

It's affecting her sleep and her diet. Increasingly it's affecting her work. Last week, for the first time in her career—no, in her *life*—she blew a deadline. Fortunately the court and her opposing counsel were decent about it (the result of ten years worth of goodwill in the system) but it's shaken her to her core.

And so last Friday she did the unthinkable: told the partnership she needs some time off. Fortunately there's a lull in her caseload and nothing on calendar for a month. She told the managing partner, her mentor and dear friend Thomas Kemp, that she needs a couple of weeks for health reasons. Tom didn't hesitate in agreeing, another result of a decade of impeccable performance. He did say, *I've noticed you looking pretty beat lately, Em-El. And I mean that out of concern. I figured you might ask for some time off after that deadline last—*

Tom, that was a once-in-a-lifetime mistake. It will never, ever happen again.

He waved a hand. *I don't give a rip about the deadline. Even if it had cost the client. But I'm glad you're taking a little leave. Start with a few weeks and let me know. You can have all the time you need.*

Mary Lee nearly burst into tears in Tom's fortieth floor corner office. The fact is she has no idea how much time she needs. After thrity-eight years of managing the clock perfectly, the irresistible motion of time has taken control of her life.

Here on the first Monday of what she's calling her sabbatical she goes about her routine as usual. Only there's nothing usual about it. She discovers how much her notion of time depended on her job. Before that it depended on graduate school, before that on university, before that on AP classes and sports, and on and on until the dawn of her memory. When she makes this discovery her first reaction is fear: she's lived this way for thirty-eight years, and suddenly because of a few random messages she's chucked it all.

And yet, as she finds herself holding a cup of coffee in her chef's kitchen with nowhere to be, looking at the Sub Zero freezer and Wolf range and marble countertops she spent weeks picking out, the only thing in the world she cares about is, *Holy God, this is the best cup of coffee I've ever had!*

She looks at her Cuisinart coffee maker, looks at her $14 a pouch gourmet coffee. It's the same stuff she's been making between 6:45 and 6:50 in the morning for ten years. But it tastes amazing, unlike any cup of coffee she's ever had. What's more, even though she's technically wasting time with this sabbatical she doesn't feel so much as a hint of unease. She can sense time passing, the sunlight growing brighter through the Frisco fog, the bluegreen digits on the oven clock flipping silently past. But she doesn't care. She only cares about the best cup of coffee she's ever had.

She says aloud to the kitchen, *Why does this coffee taste so good?!*

She's considering various answers over some scrambled eggs when the fax grinds and churns in her home office. The fear makes a go at her, but she shakes it off and walks down the hallway. Probably something from Tom that's not urgent enough to warrant an email or text. She'd asked him to keep her up to speed, lest she completely slip away.

She picks the fax off the floor. At least this time she isn't shocked. She's surprised, still, but also she's beginning to get the hang of this thing. There's no sender, no timestamp, no cover sheet. No phone number or indication that anyone or anything other than the machine itself sent the message. Just a single page with a single line in a font that reminds her of an old movie: *It's what you're doing right now.*

It's the first time a message has responded to her directly. She figures it makes sense, too, in a tinfoil hat kind of way. She's been drinking her coffee between 6:45 and 6:50 every morning for a decade, and like so much else in her life it was simply a means to an end. This is the first morning she's bothered to taste it. And it's damned good coffee. She says, *For fourteen bucks, it better be.*

Then again, maybe she just likes the taste of coffee. She wonders whether a cup of Chock Full O' Nuts would taste equally good, or a cup of Instant Yuban. The taste in her mouth, the warmth coursing into her stomach, the little jolt of energy a few minutes later. Who knew? Mary Lee really, *really* likes coffee. She just never realized it.

A jet passes overhead and she knows what comes next: She needs to fly somewhere. It doesn't matter where, she just needs to be on an airplane. Today. No, *this morning*. Like her morning coffee she's always viewed airplanes as little more than conveyance devices. The coffee conveys caffeine into her system and gives her energy, an airplane conveys her from one city to another and lets her get work done or go on the rare, and usually working, vacation. Now the thought occurs to her if she can derive such pleasure from her morning java then getting on an airplane strictly for the enjoyment of it might be positively orgasmic.

She calls out, *Where should I go?*

The fax doesn't grind, her computer doesn't flash with any mysterious destination. She looks out the window to the foggy bay half-expecting a banner plane to buzz overhead towing a personal message to her.

She laughs at herself. Whoever or whatever is behind the messages won't answer so directly. There's a spontaneity to it, almost like she needs to catch it unawares, or maybe let it catch her unawares.

Thirty minutes later she's in a Lyft Prius on the way to SFO. When the driver asks her what airline, she says, *Surprise me.*

IV

WHEN THE MAN IN the aisle seat smiles at her she feels the same giddiness—the exact same, as a matter of fact—that she felt when she heard the plane fly over her house and she knew she had to travel. She realizes she's been looking for a smile like his for a long time, maybe forever. Then again, and now she smiles herself, maybe she just started looking for it this instant. Or this morning. Or sometime last week when she decided about her sabbatical. It's all the same, and it's all relative.

Mary Lee tries to stifle a giggle and ends up snorting into her hand. She feels herself turn bright red but the man smiles the way you see people smile at works of art that catch them unawares. He hands her a handkerchief and even in her embarrassment the small act of chivalry is not lost on her, nor is his aftershave, the absence of a wedding ring, and the fact that he's the sort of man who carries a handkerchief in the first place. He says, *That's the best thing I've seen in a while.*

Mary Lee dabs her nose and eyes with the linen square. *If you think that's good, you should see me when I really get going.*

He grins. *A snorter, eh?*

I'm pretty sure at least one boyfriend left me because of it.

Now he throws his head back and laughs a full-throated laugh that feels to her like a warm ocean breeze filling the cabin. *Wow. Well, fortunately for you I have an atrocious sense of humor, and the likelihood of me making you laugh that hard on this flight is practically nil.*

She finds this difficult to believe, a suspicion he confirms with a wink. She asks, *Did you watch* Loony Tunes *when you were a kid?*

When I was a kid? I may or may not have the collection in my Netflix queue.

Do you remember a character named Pete Puma?

Of course! He imitates the Mel Blanc character, *One lump or two? He had that nasally—ohhh, I see what you're getting at.*

Mm-hmm.

That bad?

Maybe a bit worse.

That is truly amazing.

This time she successfully hides the snort. *That's one word for it.*

In that case, I'm afraid I lied to you.

You did?

I did. Can you forgive me?

That depends on the lie.

I said I wouldn't make you laugh. The truth is, I'm going to do everything in my power for the next two hours to cause you to fill this airplane with your melodious—

Don't you dare!

I'm sorry, but it's out of my hands. Let's say I'm out with the guys tonight, and I tell them about this girl I met on the flight today.

Uh-huh…

And let's say I describe her, telling them she's hands down the most beautiful woman I've ever sat next to. That's over a half million frequent flier miles talking.

We're in the same club.

Really? How many miles do you have?

Around that. But let's get back to this amazing chick you're telling your friends about.

Right! So I tell them she's stunningly beautiful, whip smart—

You don't know that. I could be a trust funder who jets around in Business Class.

Let's say I'm trusting my gut on this one. I'm telling them all this great stuff, and then I say, here's the kicker. She laughs like Pete Puma. Mary Lee feels her cheeks flush again. *Now, if I end the story there, they'll say, Swell story, Scott, and turn back to the ball game. If, however, I tell them it took two sky marshals to restrain us in handcuffs we were laughing so hard, You don't understand, guys, she damn near shook the wings off the plane! Now* THAT'S *a story.*

I have to admit, I like that your story involves handcuffs. But don't you think it would be bad for our careers to be arrested by sky marshals?

I don't know about you, but it happens I'm in the midst of a career transition. I have lots of free time.

It's Mary Lee's turn to take a long look at her seatmate. His expression doesn't change. He gazes back at her like he's been doing it his whole life. There's a slip, only this time it feels like the chain connects. Just a little at first, but it it's unmistakable. *Interesting.*

She looks out the window, and gasps. *Scott! Did you realize we'd taken off?*

I sort of half-noticed something happening out there a while ago, but I didn't pay much attention.

For a while they talk about their respective hometowns of San Francisco and Seattle (the Lyft driver that morning, shaking his head the whole way, had picked Alaska Airlines). The attendants push the meal cart past and Scott asks the one in back, *Excuse me, how long have we been in the air?*

The attendant, who has a Village People mustache and bushy black eyebrows, says, *About thirty minutes. Just under two more hours to Seattle.*

I'll be damned. The attendant raises half a caterpillar eyebrow but says nothing.

Scott looks back at Mary Lee. *Did you realize we'd been talking that long?*

She shakes her head. *I'm the one who didn't even realize we'd taken off.*

For a long time, or a short time, they don't speak. Then Mary Lee says, *I'm going to order some food. Want anything?*

Scott looks up from his book. *Sure. They usually have a food box with some hummus and crackers. Something like that would be perfect.*

You got it.

Thank you.

He reaches into his pocket but Mary Lee says, *On me, flyboy.*

How did you know that?

Know what?

You called me flyboy, but I don't remember telling you I'm a pilot.

I don't think you did. It just kind of came to me.

He raises an eyebrow and gives her the playful half-smile she'll soon come to know and love. *I can see I'm going to have to stay on my toes.*

Mary Lee smiles and looks back at the menu screen. She starts. The menu is gone, and bright pink and yellow letters say, *Let go of time, Mary Lee, and time lets go of you.*

Scott, look at my screen.

He leans over and for the first time she catches his scent full in her nose and for a moment, as they say in the old movies, she feels the vapors. *It's item number four, the rather grandiosely-named Mediterranean Feast Platter. Thank you again.*

So he doesn't see it. Which makes her wonder all over again if she sees it, if she's seen and heard any of it. She wonders what will be on that fax page when she gets home, whenever that may be.

Has something profound been happening these last two months or is she hallucinating messages from the great beyond? Either possibility requires serious examination, but as she's trying to analyze it he touches her arm. She feels another slip, the biggest one yet. Then something catches and she feels forward motion again.

Scott says, *Sorry to startle you. You were staring off into space for a few minutes there, just wanted to make sure you were still with us.*

A few minutes?

Mm-hmm.

How many?

Now Scott does a full-blown Pete Puma imitation. *Oh, four or five.*

What do you know about that, thinks Mary Lee. *Let go of time, and time lets go of you.*

She laughs again and the screen goes blank. The food menu pops back up. She orders the Mediterranean what have you for Scott, and picks a cheese plate for herself. She swipes her credit card and then turns off the screen.

She says, *So tell me about this career change, Scott.*

He smiles mysteriously. *Well, like you I practiced law at a big firm for about ten years. Last year I made a completely irresponsible decision based on a thoroughly irrational experience, and decided to follow a dream. If that isn't too much of a cliché.*

The airplane is filled with the particular light that you see only in jetliners at altitude in the morning, a light containing the energy of life against all reason and odds at 35,000 feet and 50 degrees below. The plane's red beacon flashes through a rear window and kaleidoscopes across the cabin.

It's no more of a cliché than what I'm doing.

And what's that?

Did you ever read Slaughterhouse Five?

Sure, Vonnegut. It's been a while, maybe high school, but I remember.

Remember how Billy Pilgrim used to slip into and out of time?

He gives her the look she'll come to describe as his You've Got My Attention look: He raises his eyebrows, furrows them together, then lifts his chin and squints in concentration. *I remember.*

I think I've started doing something kind of like that the last few weeks. I'm still technically a partner at Drucker, Feldman, at least as far as the firm's concerned. As for myself, as of today...

Her voice trails off.

As of today...?

As of today, she thinks, *I'm a seeker, wandering a world I think I might have to learn all over again.* She says, *As of today I guess you can call me Betty Pilgrim.*

Betty Pilgrim? Not Patti Puma?

She laughs at that. Not her full-on Pete Puma laugh, but she gives him a snort or two as preview. Her laugh makes him laugh and it's a solid minute before they stop giggling like little kids. Fortunately no sky marshals get involved.

Scott says, *So that means you got fed up with the billable hour?*

It means—I don't know what it means just yet. It means my relationship to time has changed a lot. It means here I am, right now.

There's a thump, and this time they both start. They look out the window. Red and white runway markers blur past, punctuated by blue taxiway lights. There's a roar as the pilot activates the thrust reversers. They pull off the runway.

It's happening a lot, thinks Mary Lee, *this slipping in and out of time.* Scott says, *Before I lose you in the chaos, may I have your phone number? Better yet, if you don't have plans this evening, would you join me for dinner? I know a little spot on Queen Anne Hill called the Kingfish Café. They have the best Cajun food on the West Coast, in this food snob's humble opinion.*

That's a bold statement.

It is indeed. I'd love a chance to back it up.

I do like Cajun food.

And since you're the literary type, you'll appreciate that the owners are distant relations of Langston Hughes.

The engines sigh to a stop, their work done. Mary Lee says, *Sold.*

V

SCOTT PARKED A BLOCK from the restaurant, and they strolled through the Seattle evening holding hands. It wasn't until he held the door open and she let go of his hand to step inside that she realized she was holding it in the first place.

VI

THEY'LL REMEMBER EVERY DETAIL of their first date and their first night together for the rest of their lives.

Even fifty years later (a half-century, for what it's worth) when they celebrate their anniversary with close to a hundred family members and friends, they'll say it seems like it happened yesterday.

The Devil at the Runway's End

Make him think the evil, make him think it for himself...
—Henry James

S he lay in bed next to him after she woke. It would be another couple of hours before he'd stir, and given what the morning held she let herself linger. They hadn't shown each other much affection the last six months and she wanted to get used to his feel again. She wanted him to know that after forty-three years she loved him and his body as much as ever, even if these days it was increasingly because of the memories it held.

Last night there was thunder and lightning, unusual for November in the Owens Valley. The sound like rending metal across the still-dark sky. Just two days earlier it was 80 degrees and a forty-mile-an-hour south wind sanded Bishop with dust from Owens Lake's corpse. The air tasted like alkali in the rain.

Heavy drops from the sycamore next to the house slapped the shingles. Lorna thought how it had been sixteen years since they'd reroofed the house. Sixteen years of rain, thunderstorms, dust storms, droughts, snow, blizzards. She could remember a few of them but mostly the memories were like the delirious shapes in cumulonimbus clouds, delineated not in sharp contrasts but ever-changing convections and cornices.

She did remember the first big rain after the roof was finished. The contractor's men had barely hammered the last nail into the last shingle when the heavens opened up and it rained for a week. On the fourth day the little slope in their front yard subsided, and the county sent a backhoe and dump truck to clear the street. She'd stood in knee-deep mud directing the driver along the fence line in the orange flashing light. She'd looked up at the house. The new roof shimmered in the rain light, and the living room window cast a yellow path home through the horizontal downpour. She nearly wept for joy. Vernon asked her what was wrong and she'd smiled and loved him as much in that moment as she ever had.

A couple of years later a big tree came down on the road and they'd been stuck on the hill for a week before the county—

She stopped herself. Her mind wandered like that more and more these days. Vernon joked that her brain was a three-ring circus: the real world was in the middle, but on the fringes there were always a couple of dancing bears and an elephant vying for attention. Lorna was convinced that if she was a kid today she'd be diagnosed with ADHD. Half the students in her tenth grade history class were on medication for it.

Still, as she used to point out to her fourth graders, there was a difference between thinking and stalling. Lorna knew she was stalling.

She forced herself out of bed.

It was still dark when she stood at the front window sipping a mug of coffee. She left the lights off. The habit was partly for Vernon and partly because she liked slipping into the morning at her own pace, without the disconcerting snap of electric light.

Their blue ranch-style house was two stories (really, a story and a half, the scullery and living room having no rooms above them) and formed an L with the garage. Lorna saw her silhouette against the garage door in the half-fogged glass. She thought of the construction paper silhouettes she'd taught her students to make with a flashlight and a steady hand, back when she taught elementary school. She felt a familiar pang and pushed it away. Vernon never wavered that she'd made the right decisions.

Beyond her silhouette a light drizzle flickered in the orange glow of the light at the bottom of the driveway. Ground fog hid the woods on the other side of County Road 182 and beyond them Bill McClatchy's pasture, a hundred acres of high desert grass where he grazed Angus and Blackface. Adjacent to that was the end of the Bishop Airport runway. She could just see the hangars and the planes sitting ghostlike on the tarmac. In the distance, ten miles across the valley, low-slung clouds obscured the base of the jagged eastern Sierras. She could see Mount Whitney's 14,593 feet even in the stormy pre-dawn. When you'd lived in the Owens Valley your whole life you saw the mountains in your sleep. You saw them through walls, from a thousand miles away, and in the worst gale. They were part of you.

After sixty-three years she still marveled how these late autumn mornings made her feel as though she could be anywhere, or nowhere at all.

She finished her coffee. It was a quarter past five and she was about to leave the house alone for the first time in two months.

Two months earlier, to the day, she'd been robbed at knifepoint in the house she'd shared with Vernon for thirty-seven years (even as her husband—the marine who slept so lightly during the war that a half-century later at the annual spaghetti dinner in Sacramento his surviving platoon mates still talked about how S.Sgt. Teague was never out for more than ten minutes at a stretch, and how that fact saved their bacon more than once—slumbered eight feet above her).

Her assailant had held the blade to her throat in the scullery in the spot where she now stood rinsing her mug. She touched the place on her neck and felt the cold memory of steel. She put the mug on the drying rack and walked to the parlor, willing herself not to glance at the top the refrigerator where there used to be a black and yellow Chock Full O' Nuts can with a pink index card taped to it labeled, *Adventures Fund*.

It had been the first day of real summer. California seasons are not particularly concerned with such mundane considerations as the earth's position and angle relative the sun, much less the abstractions of the Gregorian calendar.

It is possible, indeed more than likely, for there to be a two-week snow in June one year followed by a months-long winter drought the next. Even though it was still April when Lorna pushed open the back screen door that morning, she felt summer on the wind like a dried snakeskin brushing her cheek. It rasped through the sycamore branches (and there was a difference too in the way the bear paw-shaped leaves fluttered, a barely perceptible increase in their angle relative to the ground, which changed also the way the orange morning light caught them) and through the twin aspens by the chicken coops. She'd stood on the little back porch thinking, Mesquite, and the memory of summer lemonade tickled her tongue.

She'd watered the flower beds along the side fence, the herb garden in the back corner, and two big patches where they grew vegetables. She loved walking between and among the five short cornrows and inhaling the sweet smell of zucchini flowers and the tangy scent of tomatoes.

The western sky above the White Mountains glowed the color of eggplant. She carried a bucket of feed to the little chicken coop between the aspens. They'd purchased a dozen laying hens and two roosters to add to what they'd taken to calling The Farm. Vernon wanted goats and maybe even a couple of horses, and they'd agreed that chickens were a prudent first step. They built the coop out of eucalyptus and set it between the big trees so the hens would have some shade. They entered and exited at will via a little ramp.

She knew something was wrong when the hens didn't peck the air when she raised the lid of the coop. She looked at them for a moment before she realized their eyes were focused on something behind her.

Todd Cranston was waiting behind one of her beloved trees.

ભ્ર

TODD WAS A WALKING mean streak who'd landed in Lorna's eleventh grade history class five years before. According to Principal Reveta Boward he came from a broken family that dragged from one trailer camp to the next and one town to the next, Bakersfield to Bishop. He had a history of bullying, first as victim and then as perpetrator. He went to jail three times before his seventeenth birthday and was arrested another half dozen times. In an all too familiar progression he got into trouble with drugs. Which these days in rural areas like the Owens Valley meant crystal meth.

Pretty soon rumors swirled that Todd had fallen in with the valley's most notorious meth cook, Stevie Hankins. Stevie was in Lorna's class himself two years before Todd. He lived in a double-wide he'd hauled to the top of the mountain seven miles behind and 2,000 feet above Lorna and Vernon's street. He roared up the road in a bright red Ford F-250 at all hours blasting heavy metal. Twice a month a mysterious twin-engine plane landed at Bishop Airport and Stevie disappeared for three or four days. Everyone assumed he hired the plane to distribute his poison to other towns in Kern, Tulare, and Fresno counties, collectively known as the Crystal Triangle.

She had felt little empathy when Todd walked into the principal's office the Friday before the semester started, and not much more when he introduced himself with a paralyzing stutter. *Huh-huh-hu-hi, M-Ms. Tuh-Tuh-Tuh-Teague.*

He was skinny and six feet tall, with arachnid limbs and a shambling gait that reminded Lorna of a tarantula hunting at night. Despite his sharp, angular frame his features were soft, mismatched, and poorly-defined, like a Mr. Potato Head a curious child had microwaved to see what would happen. His eyes were dull blue and his skin was covered in what Lorna hoped was acne. He wore a threadbare black t-shirt with a Harley-Davidson logo, a pair of jeans with enough stains for a Rorschach test, and a pair of unlaced red Converse All-Stars. A solid layer of Mojave dust covered his face and hair. Lorna smelled something mean when he slumped into the chair next to her. *Suh-suh-suh-sorry I'm late, Mrs. Buh-Buh-Buh-Boward. Huh-had some wuh-wuh-work to fuh-fuh-fuh-fuuuhhhh-inish.*

That was about as much communication as she got out of Todd. He sat somnolently in class every day looking at her with those dull blue eyes. No, she decided one day, he was *watching* her. Studying her. Like the drug he sold Todd infected Lorna's classroom. She started thinking of him as Todd the Tumor. The worst part was he was one of the smartest kids Lorna ever encountered. He turned his work in on time, every time, as if he knew what she thought of him and gained sick pleasure defying even that. It wasn't long before she needed a glass of wine before she could bring herself to mark another red A on his work.

By the time he dropped out the week before Thanksgiving, Lorna was a bundle of raw nerves. Her students improved once he was gone but Lorna never again felt the easy joy of standing in front of her classroom. Stevie Hankins had shaken it, and Todd Cranston crushed what remained.

When she reached into the coop the chickens flapped and cackled madly. One of the hens pecked at her arm and Lorna recoiled. A hand slapped across her mouth and wrenched her neck to the right. Colors exploded in her eyes, then went gray, and of those first moments she remembered only that his hand felt like sandpaper and smelled like gasoline and black licorice.

She felt something cold against her throat. She tried to scream but the hand stayed on her mouth. A man snarled, *Sh-sh-shut the f-fuck up, tuh-tuh-teacher! You make aaaahhh sound an-an-and I'll c-c-cu-cut you. Got it-t?*

Lorna managed a wide-eyed nod. The sandpaper slid off her lips. He wedged a knee between her legs, shoved her against the chaotic coop, then half-turned her to face him. The ground wobbled.

She said, *My—my God. Todd, is it you?*

Her own voice sounded like the squeak of a mouse. He grinned a yellow and black missing tooth grin. His eyes were dead and malicious. He was high as a kite. *Guh-glad you remember mu-me.*

Todd, what are you—

Nuh-need to mu-make a wuh-wuh-withdrawal. Guh-got some buh-buh-bills.

Lorna started to say they didn't have anything, but Todd spun her around viciously and slapped his hand back over her mouth. He put his face close to her left ear. *Now, h-here's what's g-gonna hap-happen. Wuh-we're goin' in ta-ta-to yer h-h-ouse, aaaand yuh-yuh-you're gonna guh-give me every buh-buck you got. Muh-make a n-noise, I'll cuh-cut you. Under-stuh-stuh-stand?*

His spit coated her ear. Her breakfast churned in her stomach and her legs went slack. She'd have fallen if Todd hadn't held her.

She nodded helplessly.

He half-walked and half-dragged her along the path to the house muttering staccato curses about the still-cackling chickens. The familiar creak of the screen door sounded jarringly out of place, like a New Year's horn at a funeral. Todd used the knife to steer her and they walked like Siamese twins.

He whispered, *I wah-want every suh-suh-cent you got. Aaaand I'll tuh-take what-eh-eh-ever juh-juh-jewelry you got t-t-too. Muh-muh-make a ssssound a-and I'll c-c-c-c-cut,* and more spit dripped into her ear. *Guh-got it?*

She nodded again and led him to the scullery. He kept the knife in the small of her back while she stood tiptoe and retrieved the Chock Full O' Nuts can. She lost her balance and something tickled her back. Todd made a strange sound. The wound would require a dozen stitches and a tetanus shot.

Todd looked almost grateful when she gave him the can. She'd whispered, *There's almost a thousand dollars. My jewelry is upstairs, but my husband is up there sleeping.*

He seemed about to say something. For a moment he even looked like the kid that beneath it all he still was. Then he bared his drug-rotted teeth and knocked Lorna to the floor with a vicious backhand. From somewhere in the hot, rippling light like Mojave summer she heard him run out of her house and down her gravel driveway. A minute later an engine started and roared away.

She wanted to cry but she couldn't. There was only the strange shimmer. She wasn't even sure if she was still in the scullery.

Vernon didn't find her for another hour.

◦◦

AT THE FRONT DOOR Lorna caught a chill. The thermometer next to the doorbell read thirty-eight. The chill deepened to her bones and she fought the temptation to run upstairs and back to bed. Back to Vernon, her marine. Her side would still be warm and he'd tuck up against her in his sleep like he always did.

Instead she took a deep breath. It was this morning, or never. Just to the end of the driveway, she told herself. That will be a start.

She pulled on her boots and Vernon's oilcloth slicker. She paused at the Parsons table by the front door, considering the loaded military-issue .45 in the drawer.

She stepped into the cold air.

Bullfrogs croaked and from the backyard she heard one of the chickens cluck uneasily. The brick walk curved in a semicircle around a Meyer lemon tree to the corner of the garage. She walked to the tree and paused. Now that she was out here it seemed like the most natural thing in the world. She almost wanted to laugh at herself for letting it take so long. Absently, she picked a lemon while considering what to do with her rediscovered freedom.

Far down in the valley there was a flash of red lights and, a moment later, the distant peal of a train whistle. Three staccato blows in quick succession then a sustained wail. The crossing on Millwright Avenue was six miles away across Highway 16. The train's lights angled through the fog like a scythe glinting in moonlight as it swiped at the trees along the tracks. She counted silently while the crossing lights flashed. It was a short one, only forty-seven seconds. Probably fifty or sixty cars, three engines, maybe a stag. When the crossing lights blinked out, she glanced toward the little forest grove across the street.

Had it not been for a faint splotch of red light against an acacia tree in the ravine on the other side of the street Lorna never would have seen the airplane. Had the morning been ten minutes brighter she would have missed it for sure. There'd be no telling when someone would have found it.

It was there, and she saw it, recognizing instantly that a plane had gone off the runway, likely in the night during the storm. Forgetting about the significance of the morning's mission, she raced down the driveway and across the street.

She clambered down the ravine and slogged through mud and low branches and grass. Stepping around the trunk of a waterlogged oak, she saw the airplane's tail wedged into the side of the ravine about a hundred feet away. Its right wing stuck into the air like a broken arm, the engine dripping oil like blood. The plane had come to rest upside down.

She knew right away no one could have survived the crash. The airplane was facing backward and between it and the runway was a huge gash in the dirt where it had hit the ground. The impact had sheared the left engine completely off its mounts and driven a tangle of oak branches and leaves into the cabin. If the pilot and copilot were in that twisted metal wreck they were probably cut to pieces. She shuddered again and steadied herself against the tree.

There was a noise beyond the wreckage. She silently rebuked herself, *Lorna, you old fool, what if coyotes or a wildcat found the plane?* But as she listened in the stillness she realized the sound wasn't made by an animal. Someone was moaning from the airplane's cockpit.

Her own voice came out as something little more than a whisper. *Is anybody there? Hello?*

The bullfrogs momentarily ceased, the last of their calls echoing from the trees across McClatchy's field.

Lorna advanced until her eyes were level with the inverted copilot's window. She sighed with relief. There wasn't anyone in the seat. The roof was crushed in, and wires and metal hung out everywhere like the guts of a slaughtered steer. At her feet black mud glittered with chunks of shatterproof glass. She ducked under the fuselage to the pilot's side. There were just more oak leaves and branches, mud spattered on the instrument panel and floor. It smelled as though it had been there longer than a few hours.

The main cabin door was hanging open. They'd survived after all. They'd crawled out and made it to the road.

She heard the sound again. She took a step closer to the door and peered inside. An eye blinked from within the small forest inside the cabin. When it saw her it went wide. It said, *Mrs. Teague? Is that you?*

Lorna was dimly aware of a sour taste in her mouth, the croak of a bullfrog, the sun fighting through the clouds. But she couldn't feel anything, or even force any part of her body to move. She felt weightless.

The eye said, *Shit. Luh-Losin' my f-f-f-fuckin' mind. Seeing my eleventh guh-grade history teacher in a suh-swamp. G-Goddamn it. Goddamn it the fuck to Hell.*

The voice wasn't coming from the eye anymore, nor from anywhere inside the shattered truck. It came from up in the mountains, whispering like the devil wind. It started repeating,

No, no, you're ruh-real—you're really stuh-stuh standing there...
Mrs. Teague... Help me... help me... help me, becoming more
insistent, *For God's sake, why're you stuh-standing there? I'm*
buh-buh-bleeding... Help me, goddamn it! Those two muh-muh-
motherfuckers left me here to die!

The voice was silent a moment. Inside the cabin the branches
breathed weakly, leaves fluttering as they might have in a spring
breeze. Then the voice was coming from the eye again, and for the
first time in ten years Lorna heard Todd Cranston as he'd sounded
the first day of school. Before the drugs.

He said, *If you d-d-don't guh-guh-get help, I'm guh-guh-guh-*
gonna die.

Lorna heard herself reply matter-of-factly, *I expect that's true.*

S-s-so you'll huh-huh-help me?

I don't know. I haven't decided. With another chill she realized
it was true.

The eye bugged. *Duh-duh-decide what? This is l-l-l-life and*
d-d-d-death! Even yuh-you can g-g-g-get that, cuh-cuh-can't you?
I can't ffffeel anything below my wuh-waist, and everything else h-h-
huh-hurts like huh-huh-Hell. The fuh-fuh-fuck else you ni-ni-need
to know?

Don't curse, Todd.

The eye laughed. *Jesus H. Christ. Stuh-stop being a wah-wah-*
washed-up t-t-teacher long enough to c-c-c-call a fuckin' amm-
ambulance.

Lorna said, more sternly, *Todd, don't curse. It's not as simple as*
you think.

He needed to understand. She wanted to teach him. It would take time but at long last she would make him see.

Sure enough, the eye barked, *It is ssssimple. Wuh-wuh-one foot front've the other tuh-tuh-'til you get to the fuh-fuh-fuh-fuh-phone. Aaaaaand thuh-thuh-three n-numbers, n-n-nine, wuh-one, one.*

Even through his stutter he said *nine-one-one* like he was addressing an uncooperative, not-too-bright six-year-old. She wouldn't fall for his trap, not this time. She kept her composure. It made her feel powerful. She said, *It's been a matter of life and death with you for a long time now, Todd. You've been helping that Stevie Hankins make poison up in the hills. You bring it down to poison people. You don't even sell it to grown-ups who can make their own decisions, but to children who don't know any better. I can't help you unless you acknowledge what you've done.*

It was the right thing to say. She knew how to handle bad eggs. She always had, it was just that boys like Todd and Stevie had made her forget. But now he would see how much harm he'd inflicted. She'd make him see.

The eye chuckled. *If it m-m-makes you fuh-feel any buh-better, when the c-c-c-c-cops find what's in buh-buh-buh-back of this puh-puh-plane, I'll be out've b-business for a lllllllong-assed t-time. If I li-live luh-luh-long enough to g-g-g-get arrested.*

There were chemicals in Todd's tortured consonants and addiction in his agonized vowels. She imagined she was in her classroom, addressing a bad egg while her other students watched in quiet deference. Like they'd used to.

She said, *Todd, our tempers never get us anywhere. You mustn't let yours get the best of you so often. It's bad for you. Now, here you are, asking for my help, which I'm willing to give. But we won't get anywhere until you understand what got you here.*

Mrs. Teague, why d-don't you do us both a fuh-fuh-favor, and go call a f-fucking ambulance before I d-d-d-die in this duh-ditch.

The mockery was gone. The voice was low and threatening. Well, she knew how to deal with this sort of outburst. A few minutes of time to think would set him back in his place. Without another word, she stood up. She crossed back to the trail.

He called something behind her but she ignored it.

He would learn, one way or another.

She returned to the wreck ten minutes later with a blanket and a thermos of coffee. The eye blinked a few times before it focused on her. *Jesus f-f-f-f-fucking Christ, what tuh-took you so long? Where's the am-blance?*

His speech was muddy. The stuttering was nearly gone, as if his body was starting to save every ounce of energy. Even though it was getting light it was still cold, and the wind had picked up again. Lorna decided he was getting towards hypothermia. The blanket and coffee would fix that and then they could continue their conversation. He would come around. She could tell.

She leaned through the passenger door and threw the blanket over the branches. *I brought you some coffee.*

She poured a cup out of the thermos and offered it to him. The eye stared at the steaming liquid. *The fuck'm I s'pposed to d-do with this?*

I thought you'd like to stay warm while we talk.

The eye bugged out like a cartoon again, and Lorna stifled a giggle. *It looked so silly,* she thought, *dangling there in that seatbelt.*

It said, *You've lost yer shit, Mrs. Teague. You're off your fuh-fucking tuh-trolley.*

Lorna shook her head. *You cursed like that in class, remember? Oh, Todd, you were such a troubled child. But, I was right about you. Is this what you thought your life would be like? Is this what you wanted?*

A change came across the eye. The cockiness, the arrogance, vanished. For the first time that morning, it looked genuinely afraid. *You're right, Mrs. Teague. I let you have it. And I'm suh-sorry. Is that what you want?*

A wave of gratitude washed over her, but Todd just couldn't help himself. *If it muh-means so much to you I'm fucking sorry th-th-that I was too much for you to handle when I was suh-suh-seventeen fucking years old. I'm suh-sorry you were so fucking bad at your job. I'm sorry...*

His strength failed him and he took a series of gasping, rattling breaths. His breathing sounded liquid.

Lorna sighed. He'd almost fooled her, but a bad egg would always be a bad egg. And Todd wasn't just bad, he was poisoned to his core. She thought maybe if he bled a little bit more the poison would bleed out. She said, *I used to want your apology, but we're past that. You have to admit what you've done with your life. Admit how many lives you've ruined. Admit to each and every dream you've destroyed with your poison.*

The eye closed, and the branches and leaves shook. Lorna was shocked to hear quiet laughter. *You g-got no clue what you're tuh-talking about.*

Lorna said sternly, *Oh, I think I do, young man. Before you
and Stevie Hankins, my students never had the problems they have
today. They didn't get pregnant, they didn't come to class smelling of
alcohol or drugs. They didn't write obscenities on their homework or
use them in the classroom. It was your doing. You and that Stevie.
All of it.*

The eye laughed again. *Those things were going on a long
tuh-time before I came along, Mrs. Teague. Maybe you're just
g-g-getting old.*

Lorna felt herself losing control of the situation. It was like a
bad dream coming back to haunt her. *That's not true. Something
changed after you came into my life, Todd. You and that bast—
that boy, Stevie. You put a curse on my school and it's never lifted.
I've prayed for it to end, I've prayed for a return to the days when
youngsters were bright and full of hope and the only problems were
cigarettes and sometimes a girl who got into trouble. But your curse
is too strong.* She felt tears welling up in her eyes. *It's too much
for me, Todd, whatever you did to my classroom. I can't go there
anymore without seeing you. I can't walk into my backyard without
seeing you. I can't even walk into my kitchen. And that smell you
always had—*

The eye started laughing again. *I's kidding before but now I'm
sure've it. You're fucking nuh-nuts. Sure, teacher, I made you a joke.
Wuh-wasn't the time B-Brian B-B-Benjamin reminded you the Suh-
Soviet Union's guh-gone. 'Member when you thought Lincoln was
P-P-President during World War One? That's muh-my favorite.*

Lorna hadn't used corporal punishment in decades but now
she leaned into the cabin and shook the branches as hard as she

could. There was a strange sound from the eye. She was inches from it. *You're doing what you've always done, confusing the issue. You're trying to take control. But I know it wasn't me, it was you!*

Todd gasped, *Couldn't have been you n-n-n-never should've been aaaaah high school teacher in the fuckin' first place. S-s-s-sure, it was me all along. It was—*

Lorna pushed harder on the branches. She had to make him stop talking so she could finish what she had to say. She was the authority and they wouldn't get anywhere until he accepted that.

She pushed on the branches.

She pushed one branch in particular and it went forward, down into the cab, down toward the eye.

It cut his scream short.

Lorna was almost screaming now herself, a tone of voice she'd never used before in class. *Children were angels. They were innocent vessels, waiting for their teachers and parents to fill them up with goodness. Everything came apart when you came along. The children weren't good anymore. Parents didn't care anymore. The school wasn't a sacred place anymore. My class wasn't. All because of you!*

A sound like mud gurgled from the branches and she let go. The eye let out an almost imperceptible noise, like the sound of a plastic ketchup bottle.

Her voice was raw. *Todd, do you understand everything I just said? Will you admit what you've done at last?*

There was no reply. She reached, slowly, through the branches toward where the eye had been, half expecting something to reach out and drag her into the airplane. But nothing happened. She pushed deeper and deeper, until she felt Todd's skin. She pressed and heard what sounded like an exhalation.

She stepped back from the door. *I hope that didn't hurt, Todd, I just wanted to make sure you were still there. I'll get the ambulance now. I'm glad you listened. I think we understand each other now. I think now maybe you'll change your ways, won't you?*

The eye didn't speak.

Suddenly Lorna wanted to be as far away from Todd Cranston and the crashed plane as she could. She scrambled, stumbling, up the ravine and through the grass and mud to the road. Oak branches tore at her face. She ran faster than she'd run in years, maybe even in her entire life.

She flew through the door and flung open the Parson's table drawer. The black pistol, and all its power, lay on a white cloth like some sort of holy relic whose power until now she'd only dimly comprehended.

Vernon was at the kitchen table when the front door slammed open hard enough to crush the stopper and knock a chunk of plaster out of the wall. He took one look at Lorna clawing at the drawer where they kept his old marine-issue .45, and jumped to his feet. His bowl of cereal crashed to the floor and he ran to her. *My God, Lorna, what's the matter? Have you been crying? Lorna, honey, sit, sit. Just calm down and tell me what happened.*

He took the gun out of her hand and put it back in the drawer.

Lorna looked at Vernon. It was as if she hadn't seen him in twenty years. He looked younger. He looked like the photograph on the mantel, in his uniform the day he received his stripes. She almost cried at how handsome he was.

Of course Vernon looked younger. The curse had been lifted. She couldn't wait to look in the mirror.

She started to tell him what had happened in the ravine but when she opened her mouth the only thing that came out was laughter. They stood there in the doorway, fog swirling into the living room, and Lorna laughed and laughed until tears ran down her face.

Canvas and Cables

*I*t's not flying anymore. Hasn't been for thirty years. I'm not a pilot, Consuela, I'm a damned IT manager at a multinational corporation.

Consuela leaned on her side of the bar. *Not from the way people look at you, you're not. You're larger than life. You're biased.*

How's that, Capitan?

You have a crush on me.

Consuela rolled her eyes. In her dark pupils Trent saw the restaurant's front door open. He knew without looking over his shoulder it was Fernando. The floor under Trent's barstool vibrated as Consuela's cousin strode into El Cholo Taqueria, settled at his usual spot next to Trent, and put his cowboy hat on the bar. He exchanged a kiss with Consuela then clapped Trent's shoulder with his solid farmer's son's hand. *Hola, Cabron. How's it hanging?*

Down to my kneecaps and mad as Hell.

Fernando bellowed his big Mexican laugh and Trent caught a whiff of avgas, white dust pesticide, and pipián verde. *L'eau du Fernando.* He was the veteran marine who flew crop dusters for a dozen ranches in Ventura and Oxnard. Trent Wilcox was a retired air force pilot who flew 747s for Delta Airlines and never smelled like anything besides Old Spice and, during weeks he wasn't flying, Four Roses bourbon. It was his inebriant of choice since he read somewhere it was Faulkner's drink.

Consuela poured a tumbler of Don Julio over ice and set it on a coaster in front of her cousin. *How was your day, primo?* Trent's Spanish wasn't terrible but they usually spoke English.

Fernando took a swig of tequila and Consuela refilled his glass. *At sea level, a pain in the ass. Up in the air, blessed and beautiful.*

Trent chuckled. *A day on the ground's a wasted day.*

Fernando said, *And yet here you sit.*

He slugged back the second tequila and Trent made a run at his fourth bourbon. Consuela shook her head. *The way you boys drink.*

If my cousin didn't own a bar I couldn't afford to drink so much. You're a godsend, Consuela.

Trent watched them exchange a look. Consuela had been sober nine years, since her husband Abel drank himself to death. Jokes about booze fell pretty flat with her. There was a tense moment and then she said, *Trent has some extra days on the ground this time.*

Fernando raised an eyebrow. *Aye? What's that about?*

Trent gave Consuela a look that said, *Thanks a lot.* He was in no mood for this conversation after the week he'd had. He focused on his glass.

Fernando prodded, *You got some free time, does that mean you're finally gonna take me up on my offer?*

Not now, Fernando. Can't you see I'm trying to get drunk in peace?

There's nothing peaceful about you when you're drunk.

Says the pot to the kettle.

Fernando snorted. *One night, and you never let me live it down.*

You drove your truck in to a eucalyptus tree.

That's right, and a good thing, too. Otherwise I might have made it to your place and finished the fight.

Uh-huh.

Fernando said to his cousin, *He been like this all afternoon?*

He's hardly said a word. Just reading his book and ignoring me.

Fernando picked up the paperback next to Trent's glass. He said, *Too heavy for me, man.* Light in August? *No wonder you're depressed. My favorite's* The Reivers. *But if I have enough tequila I might pick up* As I Lay Dying *and cry a little bit over mi madre, God rest her.*

Trent looked at his friend. *Five years and you're still full of surprises, Fernando. I didn't know you liked literature.*

Consuela said, *He thinks all we read is* The Bear Prince *and* The Gypsy Queen.

Tsk-tsk, just another racist gringo.

Trent said, *What can I say, you know I can't stand Mexicans. It's why I spend nearly all my free time here. I'm a masochist.*

Perhaps one day you'll learn to love us. Anyway, amigo. You have free time, so come with me just once. I'll never bother you again.

Why don't I believe that?

Fernando grinned. *Because I'm lying.*

Trent pleaded, *Consuela, do something.*

She moved down the bar to fill a server's drink order. *I don't get involved when the boys argue.*

Trent called, *You only say that when you're taking Fernando's side.*

She waved a hand in the air and set to work on three pitchers of margaritas and a bucket of Bohemias.

Fernando was still smiling.

Trent said, *What?*

You two...

Fernando, amigo, don't start. I'm begging you. The day I've had. The month I've had.

She's worried about you.

I can take care of myself.

We're both worried about you, bro.

Can we talk about football?

When my friend's in pain I can give a shit about the pinche Raiders. They've broken my heart enough, anyway. Fernando reached over the bar and grabbed the bottle of Don Julio. He poured two fingers and took a sip. *She can't hear us. So tell me what's going on.*

Trent sighed. Talking around Fernando was like talking around an Abrams Tank. So he told his friend the story. Consuela drifted by from time to time but mostly kept her distance. In the five years they'd known him Trent and Fernando had become like brothers. It made sense, Trent was the only child of an abusive father and Fernando was the youngest of four brothers and the only one who'd never been to prison. These days he only saw his dad at family funerals. Consuela gave them their space to talk as brothers. Besides, she had a pretty good idea what was going on with the man she not-so-secretly loved.

Trent told Fernando what Fernando knew, that he never wanted to be anything but a pilot. They shared that passion. But then Trent admitted his passion was turning into the problem. There were really two Trent Wilcoxes: there was Captain Wilcox of Delta Airlines, who as a 747 captain had one of the few jobs that still inspired awe in the jaded age of modern air travel. He was Captain Wilcox of the reassuring baritone that came over the PA as you hoisted your carry-on into the overhead compartment, *Good afternoon, ladies and gentlemen, from the flight deck*, a voice that in its first syllable conveyed the most important message an airline captain ever delivers to his or her passengers: *You're in good hands, folks.*

Captain Wilcox was a minor legend among the elite pilots who flew some of the biggest airplanes in the world. The airplanes he flew seemed to behave like extensions of his body. In 2006 he'd landed a 747-8 in Taipei, Taiwan in a seventy-knot crosswind and near-zero visibility with two engines out, a damaged left stabliator, and all of 15 percent of the plane's hydraulic pressure remaining. After the longest inquiry into a nonfatal incident in aviation history, the Taiwanese and American investigators and Boeing engineers concluded that what he'd done was a physical impossibility.

Captain Wilcox remembered every flight he'd ever taken and could call up details on cue. Ask him where he was on June 25, 1987 and without a beat he'd tell you he was at 36,000 feet over the Aleutian Islands in an F-16C Fighting Falcon intercepting a Soviet

Tu-26 Bear bomber. He'd add that the weather was clear with a few cirrus clouds, winds aloft were twenty knots out of the northwest, and his wingman was Stephanie "Slingshot" Singleton. He'd even include the conversation they'd had with the Soviet crew in sign language and the number of times they flipped each other the bird. This was Captain Wilcox of the gleaming epaulettes, razor-sharp blue uniform, and commanding stride through international terminals from LAX to Moscow, JFK to Taipei.

Then there was Trent, a fifty-three-year-old bachelor with two ex-wives to go with a serious drinking problem, a severe sleep problem, a desperate libido problem, and a grinding sense that everything he'd done with his life to date was futt-bucking wrong. Two divorces and a fondness for the horses had pretty well ruined him financially. He lived in a one-bedroom apartment two blocks from the 10 freeway in Temple City and drove a dinged-up fifteen-year-old car he parked in the long-term lot at LAX so his fellow aviators wouldn't see it.

Captain Wilcox had 300-page flight manuals and hundreds of Victor airways committed to memory. Trent misplaced his car keys and wallet at least once a day in his 500 square foot shoebox. Captain Wilcox had never been late a day in his life. Trent was lucky if he was on time one time out of ten. The most important difference was that Captain Wilcox never drank more than a beer with dinner and never within twenty-four hours of flying. Trent marinated his liver in bourbon at every opportunity.

He spent his off-duty days sipping Four Roses and reading William Faulkner at El Cholo. Trent liked Faulkner because of the writer's lifelong fascination with aviation and because he was the only man Trent had encountered, living or dead, who shared his notions about just how deep the rabbit hole of the human psyche really is. He liked El Cholo because of Consuela and Fernando and because it was eighty-four years old. The menu had barely changed since Kennedy was president and the décor would have made a zoot suit kid feel right at home. Consuela was probably the only restaurant owner in California who hadn't installed a blaring flat-screen TV in the bar and plastered her windows with stickers of websites that loved El Cholo. She played classic mariachi music and big band crooners on an old jukebox and got her business from people who knew where to find the best Mexican food in the valley. When he stepped from the small eucalyptus-shaded parking lot on Temple Avenue into the cool, dark adobe restaurant and the heavy oak door closed he felt peaceful. There weren't many places left in the world that gave him that feeling. Trent had come to think of El Cholo as his panic room from the modern world.

And damn, did he need one of those. But even in the safe confines of Consuela's restaurant, he was a bit on the freaked out side of things this afternoon.

Trent had started making appearances on Captain Wilcox's flight decks.

He told Fernando it started three and a half weeks ago. He was over the south Pacific en route from Hong Kong to Sea-Tac at 36,000 feet and 540 knots indicated when suddenly he'd tasted bourbon in his mouth and for a few seconds lost all sense of where he was and the plane he was flying. A week later at 37,000 and 590 knots over Greenland he took a swallow of cranberry juice that tasted like Four Roses and nearly puked on the instrument panel. The same head-spinning feeling hit him. It lasted longer the second time.

He hadn't said anything to his crews, much less reported the incidents to the airline as per regulations. *Captain pushing fifty-five experiencing medical episodes* was longhand for *early retirement.* And these days flying was the one thing standing between him and complete collapse. Besides, Captain Wilcox had 41,973 hours of flight time including fifty-three combat missions over Iraq in the Gulf War as a Weapons Systems Officer in an F-15E Strike Eagle. He'd been wounded in the first night of the air war, recovered in record time, and been back on flight duty within a month. Captain Wilcox would be damned if he'd let some FAA white coat tell him when to hang up his spurs.

Trent wasn't so sure.

He told Fernando today was the worst one yet. After ten hours in the air from Tokyo they were headed for the north forty-five approach to LAX, when Captain Wilcox's mouth swirled with bourbon again. He'd gagged, given the plane to his copilot Shelly Mumm, and barely made it to the forward lavatory before his salmon lunch and what tasted like a half bottle of Four Roses came back for an encore. When he looked in the mirror he'd seen not Captain Wilcox's calm, clear-eyed face but Trent's bloodshot eyes and puffy, burst capillary visage. He splashed water on his face and slapped himself silly then sat down on the john and tried deep breathing exercises. Nothing helped. He went back to the flight deck as Trent. He felt drunk and was sure First Officer Mumm would smell booze in the cockpit. When she gave him a quizzical look, he'd said lamely, *Lunch isn't sitting too well. You take us in, just to be on the safe side.*

When he pulled out the checklist, First Officer Mumm chuckled. *You must really be nailed. Wait 'til people hear Captain Wilcox took out a checklist.*

Trent started to reply but that was when the second half of his lunch came up. He managed to get his head down and puke on the floor instead of the instruments, which was about the only break he would get.

First Officer Mumm said, *Captain!*

The floor and radio console spun before his eyes and the mere thought of talking agonized his guts. Hell, *breathing* nearly brought up breakfast. A mushroom and spinach omelet was on deck in his stomach.

He pursed his lips and managed a sound like, *Puh.*

First Officer Mumm said, *Sorry, Captain, this is gonna cause a ruckus. But you are a very sick man.*

She keyed her mic. *Pan-Pan, Pan-Pan, Pan-Pan, Los Angeles Approach, Los Angeles Approach, Los Angeles Approach. Delta eight-seven-two heavy, thirty miles north over Point Mugu. Our captain is experiencing a medical emergency, nature unknown. Request an expedited landing and paramedics on the tarmac, over.*

In his headphones Trent heard, *Delta eight-seven-two heavy, LA. Approach. Understand you have a medical emergency. You're cleared direct to Runway Seven Left. Descend and maintain five thousand feet until the Santa Monica VOR then enter left downwind at your discretion and contact LA Tower on point two five. There* followed a series of rapid-fire instructions to other planes to get out of the way.

Trent groaned. Ruckus, indeed. Shit show was more like it. Airspace over major cities and international airports are places of intensive coordination and choreography. An emergency call didn't just screw up that coordination, it could ripple up and down the West Coast and potentially the whole country.

The floor mercifully slowed down. Trent tested himself with a few deep breaths. It felt okay. Nothing was spinning anymore. He put his hands on the base of the instrument panel. *Okay. Okay. I think I'm all right.*

His copilot didn't answer. She was busy making sure a 700,000 pound airplane with 407 souls on board got onto the ground safely and lickety-split. Trent picked up his slightly puke-spattered checklist, but without taking her eyes off the sky she said, *Don't worry about it, Captain. We got Jenna.*

Jenna was a new automated voice system the airline was trying out, programmed with every checklist and procedure in the manual for situations like this one. As Trent, starting to feel like Captain Wilcox again, sat with his head back and eyes closed a breathy female voice began the pre-landing checklist. *Exterior lights on.*

Trent managed to chuckle. Jenna was named for the porn star, Jenna Jameson, because, well, she sounded like she was doing something very naughty as she ran through the checklist. *Approach briefing complete. I've slipped off my panties and I'm soooo wet.*

Trent said, in a voice that sounded reassuringly like Captain Wilcox, *We got time for one of the attendants bring us some paper towels? And perhaps a hose?*

First Officer Mumm smiled at the *Monty Python* reference. She picked up the phone on the back of the center console and rang the main galley. *Hey, Barb, would you come up to the cockpit with a whole bunch of towels, double time? We had a gastrointestinal mishap. Thanks, doll.*

His eyes still closed Captain Wilcox said, *You know, if I called a flight attendant doll, I'd probably get sued.*

Yeah, I know. It's so tough to be a man.

I might be violently ill but I still know sarcasm when I hear it, First Officer Mumm.

Good, 'cause I was laying it on pretty thick. You have a reputation for a lot of things but a grasp of the ironic isn't among them. Now shut up, I'm flying a great big goddamned plane.

Jenna said, *Flaps ten degrees. Mmmm, landing configuration gets me hot.*

Barbara knocked on the cockpit door. When Captain Wilcox opened it the head flight attendant covered her mouth and nose and gasped, *Good grief you guys! You having a party in here?*

He snatched the rags and spray bottle from her. *Thank you, Barbara, that will be all.* He closed the door before she could say or see anything else.

By the time they were on downwind, he felt as though nothing had happened. He'd done a yeoman's job of cleaning the cockpit. First Officer Mumm told the tower they'd be okay with a medical crew at the gate, no need to scare people with flashing emergency equipment lights and a mid-taxiway stop. They made a thoroughly uneventful landing, and First Officer Mumm announced cheerfully on the PA that they were ten minutes ahead of schedule. She left out the why.

At the gate Captain Wilcox discretely exited with the First Class passengers and caught a golf cart inside the terminal that whisked him to the airport medical clinic.

The doctor was perplexed. She said, *You say you puked your guts up twice out of nowhere and then you were absolutely fine five minutes later? Something food-borne is my best guess. If I were you, from now on I'd avoid airline fish. Still, I'm going to recommend you stay off flying duty for two weeks. Sorry, Captain. You'll have to schedule an exam with your aviation doc in the next forty-eight hours.*

Delta Airlines didn't even wait for that. He was halfway home when his cell phone rang. The regional director told him his flight status was suspended indefinitely, pending a full medical exam, a battery of tests, and a management review. Trent didn't argue. He couldn't argue. The manager, Jack Forsland, said, *Good luck, Captain. I'm sure you'll be back in no time.*

A bolt of finality went through Trent when the line went dead. He felt like he might never talk to anyone at Delta Airlines again. As he merged on to the 110 freeway and headed for the San Gabriel Valley a more profound reality set in: for the first time in thirty-five years Trent Wilcox couldn't fly airplanes. It felt like a sledgehammer to his balls.

Which is why, he told Fernando, he was two-thirds of the way through a bottle of Four Roses at El Cholo, feeling like the tenuous balance between his two lives was hurtling from its fulcrum.

Fernando, who'd nearly cleared the bottle of tequila himself, looked at Trent for a long moment. When he was drunk his Oaxacan accent was especially strong. *Listen to me seriously. I know when my brother is in need and I also know what will get you fixed. I'll pick you up tomorrow morning at seven a.m. sharp.*

Trent put his head in his hands. *Jesus Cristo, Fernando, I'm getting sick just thinking about it. You want to stick a jalapeño up my ass while you're at it?*

If you don't ask my cousin on a proper date soon I will. But first we need to fix you up. He stood and put on his hat. Fernando was the most dignified drunk Trent had ever met. *Seven a.m. You better start taking aspirin right now, hombre. No is not an option this time.*

Fernando—

I said no is not an option. You need to remember what it's like to be a pilot.

I have a pretty good idea about piloting. I have forty-one thousa—

Yeah, I know. Forty thousand-whatever hours. Big man. When's the last time you flew something that wasn't a big plastic computer?

That one stung. Actually, it hurt like Hell. It took Trent by surprise. He said defensively, *Look, I appreciate the romance of flying and all that, but it's not what I need right now. I'm beginning to think what I need is AA.*

Fernando snorted. *You're not an alcoholic, you're a drunk. Alcoholics need group therapy and years of counseling. Drunks need to be reminded of who they are and why they started drinking in the first place.*

Trent took another sip. *That's an awfully fine hair you're splitting.*

And you're walking a very fine line. See you in the morning. Hasta mañana.

This time Fernando didn't wait for Trent's answer. He went to the other end of the bar and hugged his cousin goodbye. Trent saw them exchange whispers and something inside him felt vaguely violated. As much as he loved them he would not let even Fernando and Consuela into Captain Wilcox's world. Now Fernando seemed determined to barge his way in, invited or not. After Fernando left, Trent looked helplessly at Consuela. She smiled mysteriously and shook her head. *Great,* he thought, *not even Consuela, the only person on planet Earth who could—sometimes—talk sense into her cousin, was going to bail him out this time.* He finished the bottle and stumbled home.

Sure enough, Trent's phone rang at 5:45 the next morning, and sure enough the caller ID said Fernando Barragan. As it rang through his headache he considered not answering. It kept ringing and he considered putting it on silent. It rang some more and he considered throwing it against the wall. Of course if he did that Fernando would be pounding on his door in a half hour.

He thought, *Ok, amigo, ok. You win.* The irresistible force prevails over the immovable object. Just this once. He fumbled on the nightstand for his phone and tapped the answer icon. *Thought you said seven.*

I'm picking you up at seven. I thought I'd give you some time to drink some water and take a few more aspirin.

Thanks, I think.

De nada.

Do I get to know what this is all about? We going cropdusting?

You'll know in two hours. Now get your gringo ass out of bed. We have a big day ahead.

Fernando—

Fernando clicked off.

At precisely 7:00 he knocked on Trent's door. He was wearing jeans, a black cowboy shirt embroidered on the collars and shoulders, and his cowboy hat. He handed Trent a bottle of water, a small Tupperware container, and a roll of warm tortillas. The container was hot to the touch. He said, *Jazmin got up at five a.m. to cook you her special Menudo. You can thank her this weekend. You look better than I expected.*

I know how I look, and I don't want to know what you expected. Let's go.

They got into Fernando's truck, a red 1949 Chevy five-window pickup that was as cherry as any vehicle in Southern California. He'd seen it as a rusting wreck in a field outside Corona the day he was discharged from the marines. He figured it was an omen and he bought it on the spot with the last $500 to his name. He spent two years rebuilding it and when it was done an appraiser valued it at $28,000. Fernando was a genius with all things mechanical and the older the machine, the greater his passion.

They didn't talk as Fernando got onto I-5 north. In Santa Clarita they picked up Highway 14 and headed for Mojave. Trent sipped the hot spicy soup and watched the sprawl give way to dusty oak and sage covered hills. A few miles north of Edwards Air Force

Base, Fernando exited the freeway and they climbed along a two-lane street into the desert foothills.

The Menudo started doing its work. Trent asked, *You taking me into the mountains to rediscover my love of flying or to put me out of my misery?*

Fernando rolled down his window and took a deep breath of desert air. *All right, I'll give you a hint. For the last six months I've been learning to fly a new airplane. I was just certified two weeks ago, when you were in Singapore, I think.*

What kind of plane?

Fernando grinned widely. *That, amigo, is part of the surprise.* The street turned into a narrow one-lane dirt road. *Get ready to go back in time.*

They crested a hill and Trent realized his friend meant it almost literally. A small grass airstrip lay nestled in a long, narrow valley. It looked as if it had been there a hundred years and hadn't changed much in all that time. No tower, no runway lights, no taxiways or tarmac. The runway wasn't marked. It was just a broad swath of close-cut grass surrounded by taller grass, then by oak trees and sage brush and the desert mountains. There were windsocks at either end of the airstrip and a half-dozen old wooden hangars on the far end of the field that somehow seemed like they had just been built. It looked like a place where a barnstormer might land any minute.

Trent said, *I'll be damned. Thought I knew every airport and airstrip in California. What field is this?*

We call it Valley Home.

We?

Those of us who know about it. There are ten planes left here. There used to be many more. This was one of the first airfields in California. The FAA decommissioned it sometime in the sixties and it hasn't showed up on any WAC chart or sectional since.

A ghost airport.

And yet very, very much alive. There are only ten planes but they're special airplanes with long histories. The newest of them is a forty-seven Aero Commander that used to belong to Howard Hughes.

Did he build the field?

Fernando shook his head. *No one knows who built it. But Hughes filmed part of* Hell's Angels *here.* He pointed at a hangar. *Pancho Barnes kept her Ghost Ship in that hangar for a few months. Now there's a P-38 in there called Kandy Kim.*

Trent gaped. Telling a pilot there was a Lightning at your airport was like telling a jazz fan you had one of Duke Ellington's pianos. For a moment he felt like a giddy little kid. *A P-38? Seriously? There are only a dozen left flying.*

Fernando winked. *Thirteen, actually. Kandy Kim is—well, maybe someday you'll get a chance to see her. Anyway, many great pilots have come through here over the years. Bob Hoover taught aerobatics at Valley Home in a Stearman in the forties and Amelia Earhart used the field when she was practicing for her Atlantic flight, to avoid the press. Lindbergh had a plane here and so did Bessie Coleman. Yeager, Rickenbacker, Cohcran, Doolittle, Quimby, Raiche, they all came through here one time or another. A few years ago Neil Armstrong, Buzz Aldrin, and John Glenn showed up with their grandkids and spent an afternoon shooting model rockets into the sky.*

Even Captain Wilcox would have admitted this was a pretty cool airstrip.

They bounced over the grass toward the first hangar. Fernando stopped the truck and killed the engine. *And now, amigo, we go back in time.*

Trent felt like they'd stared doing just that the moment they saw the strip. He helped Fernando haul open the hangar door.

And then his jaw dropped a second time. There were two airplanes inside and both were more than seventy-five years old. One was a red and orange 1937 Beech Staggerwing, a single-engine biplane that most pilots consider one of the most beautiful airplanes ever built. It was modern for its era, with a 200 mph cruise speed, retractable landing gear, and a cabin class interior. Its most distinctive feature was its negative wing stagger: its upper wing was set back farther on the fuselage than the lower wing, giving the plane a graceful forward sweep that made it look like it was cruising at 10,000 feet sitting on the ground.

The other was an even rarer bird: a silver twin-engine Lockheed Model 12 Electra monoplane, the kind of plane Amelia herself flew on her round-the-world attempt. Its two massive radial engines nearly dwarfed the cockpit and cabin and gave the plane a muscular, powerful stance. Trent, who suddenly felt Captain Wilcox's mind at work, knew this plane was even rarer than the P-38 hidden in one of the other hangars. There were only two left flying in the world.

As if reading his thoughts, Fernando said, *The only people who know about this airplane are the ones who know about Valley Home.*

We spent seven years rebuilding her, rivet by rivet, panel by panel. She's only been airworthy the last six months.

We?

The fellows who maintain the field and the planes. Depending on how things go today I'm going to introduce you at our next gathering.

You're being awfully mysterious, amigo.

Have I ever steered you wrong?

So long as I keep you away from eucalyptus trees, no.

Pendejo de mierda.

Seriously, Fernando, these are the most beautiful airplanes I've ever seen. I mean—they're exquisite! Trent walked around both planes, nose to tail. These weren't just airplanes, they were works of art, and joyous ones at that. *God, I wish we still made airplanes like these.* He was feeling more like a little kid every minute.

Fernando chuckled. *Consuela thought you'd say something like that.*

Consuela?

She comes out and helps from time to time. He shook his head. *I don't understand why she never learned to fly herself. She's a mysterious woman, my cousin. And of course I do not have to tell you how much she cares for you.*

Trent paused next to the Staggerwing's silver propeller blade. *I guess you don't.*

She says you are an old soul who is lost in the modern world. There are two people named Trent Wilcox, she tells me. There's the man who comes to her restaurant because it's eighty years old, reads books by writers who've been dead forty years, and asks her to play music that has not been on the radio in half a century. Then there is the man who spends his days flying giant plastic computers around in the sky. She thinks one of you has the potential to be very happy, but the other is keeping both of you very sad.

Trent shook his head. *That's one insightful relative you have, Fernando.*

Don't I know it.

Do you know why I became a pilot, Fernando? He held up two fingers. *Two reasons. First, there's the reason I give everyone who ever asks me: my dad and grandfather were pilots. Grandpa flew P-51s in Europe in World War Two, and Pop flew F-4s in Vietnam. So I rode shotgun in F-15s in the Gulf and now I fly 747s.*

You've told me that. I always thought they forced you into the family business.

Trent snorted. *My old man didn't give a damn what I did with my life. You don't understand, Fernando. My dad and grandfather, they were like gods to me, but Pop was like one of the Greek or Roman gods who took out his rage on human beings. I remember when I was five years old and Mom took me to an airshow at El Toro. Dad was performing in a Super Sabre. It was the first time I ever saw him fly.*

You must have been proud. While they talked Fernando started preflighting the Electra. He climbed on the right wing and popped the cowl.

Proud? No. I was scared out of my mind. The jet was so damned loud I thought the sound would rip my guts out. When I saw the afterburners I thought his plane was on fire and he was going to crash. I stood right in the middle of the VIP section with the other military families and cried my eyes out. In front of my parents' friends, my dad's squadron mates, I begged my mommy to take me out of there. Then I pissed myself. Mom dragged me to the car when dad was in the middle of a split-s.

Fernando replaced the cowl on the engine and moved to the other wing. *You were just a boy.*

Trent climbed onto the Staggerwing's lower wing and leaned against the fuselage. He realized he hadn't sat on an airplane wing in years. Maybe decades. The canvas and metal felt good. No— they felt real. *Yeah, I was just a boy, and that night when Dad got home he told me if I did something like that again he'd whip me raw. I knew from experience it wasn't a bluff. Then he said, No son of mine is going to be a coward.*

Up on the Electra's big wing Fernando leaned against the pilot's window and faced Trent. *My old man was a bastard like that, too. When I was twenty he actually told me I was a pussy because I'd never been in prison like my brothers.*

We should get them together sometime.

Yes, lock them in a room with a bottle of tequila and hope they beat each other senseless. It might do them both some good.

Trent smiled at that. *Anyway, I followed in their footsteps because one day when I was sixteen years old I got the damned fool idea to take a flying lesson. June seventh, nineteen seventy-one. I'd never been flying except in airliners, and I wanted to try it just once. I was scared shitless but I had to prove I wasn't a coward. That was the first time I felt it.*

Felt it?

The second reason I became a pilot. The real reason. The reason that has nothing to do with my dad or grandfather. It was like falling in love, the first time I pulled back on the stick and felt myself leave the earth. Magic. I had my license five months later, the day after my eighteenth birthday. November twenty-ninth, nineteen seventy-one. For a few years, before I joined the Air Force because I thought I could finally beat my old man at his own game, I loved flying more than life itself. I loved Cessnas, Pipers, Beechcrafts. I loved Avgas and the smell of the inside of an airplane. I loved the sound of a Lycoming engine…

Trent realized he was talking a mile a minute. He paused. *The problem is that every day since then I've loved it a little less.*

Fernando frowned. *Give me a break, amigo. You've flown the fastest fighter jet in the world and now you fly the biggest airliner in the world. You're probably one of the best pilots around and you're telling me you don't like flying.*

Technically I didn't fly F-15s, I was a back-seater. And like I was telling Consuela yesterday, the planes I fly these days are just big goddamn computers. Do you know a 747-8 has one hundred forty-three miles of wires in it? Where's the soul in that?

A smile spread slowly across Fernando's face and he started chuckling. Then he was laughing, a big, bellowing laugh that shook the hangar's wooden walls. He clapped his hands together and smacked the Electra's wing. *Madre de Dios! Consuela, oh Consuela! Ha!*

What am I missing, Fernando?

My friend, you are not missing a thing. You are getting a great gift, only you don't know it yet. You may be an old soul, Trent, but compared to Consuela you're a child. We all are.

Fernando jumped off the wing. He took a small envelope out of his pocket and handed it to Trent. *Consuela wanted me to give this to you before we took off this morning. I don't know what she wrote but I can guess. Read it tonight when you get home.*

Trent took the envelope. Next, Fernando fished something out of his other pocket. He held up two key chains, each with a single key dangling from it. *And these are from me.*

Wait. Are those—

Sí.

This week has been surreal, Fernando, but now you've got me at a total loss.

It is quite simple. We are going flying.

I got that part.

We will go to Catalina and have buffalo burgers at the airport restaurant. There we will discuss the details of our partnership.

You're moving too fast for me. And even after Jazmin's Menudo I might still be a little drunk.

I'm offering you a partnership in these airplanes.

For the first time that morning Trent was deflated. *Fernando, brother, you have no idea how broke I am.*

Oh, I have an idea. And the partnership isn't about money anyway. Do you think a crop duster can afford these kinds of toys?

So who owns them? How many partners are there?

Fernando gave him another one of his mysterious grins. *You still have a lot to learn about airplanes, amigo. I'll tell you everything en route.*

They attached handles to the Electra's main wheels and pulled it into the sunlight, then Fernando opened the main door and folded down the stairs. Trent followed him inside.

The first thing he noticed was that it smelled like an airplane. Not like the sterile plastic and glass cockpit of a modern jetliner but like a real, live machine. Trent felt like he was seventeen and climbing into that Piper Cub for the first time, with all the anticipation of a young man on the cusp of something extraordinary, perhaps even magical. He actually felt a lump in his throat when Fernando called, *Clear prop!* (a pilot's force of habit, there wasn't anyone else within ten miles of the propellers) and fired up the engines. He felt and heard and smelled every detail. He actually giggled like a kid as they bounced over the rough field. He realized he'd forgotten what a real airplane felt like.

As Fernando advanced the throttles and they accelerated bouncing and bounding down the rutted field he felt positively exuberant.

And then he felt it. The moment the wheels left the earth, the moment the last of the Electra's weight transferred from its tires to its wings, he felt an instant of weightlessness. In that moment, Trent decided that Captain Wilcox was going to retire from Delta Airlines. As they climbed through the calm morning air and Fernando leveled just 500 feet over the hills, Trent realized that Captain Wilcox had memorized all those checklists and Victor airways and every detail of every flight for the same reason that Trent drank. It was a way to dull the pain, to focus his mind on anything besides the thing he knew (and, as they chased a herd of white-tailed deer across a hilltop, he realized he'd always known): he'd been flying the wrong planes all these years. Now that he was once again in the right kind of plane he felt happier than he had—

well, since those few precious years when he was a young man just discovering the magic of aviation.

He turned to his friend. *Fernando, I don't know what else you have in store, but you've just made me about the happiest son of a bitch on the face of the earth. Or above it for that matter. I never realized it, but it's so simple!*

And yet completely mysterious.

Amen, brother. Now tell me about these fellows.

Fernando flashed his mysterious grin once more. As they climbed into the western sky and chased the clouds to Catalina, Fernando began. *I'll tell you all about them in time. But first you need to hear about Kandy Kim…*

છ

THAT EVENING AT HOME, Trent collected all the full and half-full bottles of booze secreted in various places and dumped them down the drain. Then he called Jack Forsland and left a voicemail announcing his intent to resign from Delta Airlines. Finally, he poured himself a glass of orange juice and sat down at his table with Consuela's letter.

Halfway through he was laughing and crying. He said aloud, *Consuela, oh Consuela!*

He dialed the phone number at the end of the letter.

The Ballad of Kandy Kim, Part 3

As we prepare for our final landing there are a few details left to take care of. It's presumptuous, we know, given how much of your time you've given to our bards and raconteurs, but we'd like to end this little volume of flying stories with a recommendation.

Before we do, there's a final part to the story of Kandy Kim. We mentioned that there were other airplanes in World War II that performed heroic feats without the benefit of a pilot. It shouldn't come as a surprise that the clan couldn't hear these stories and not investigate. Over the years they've talked with pilots and ground crews, engineers and designers. They discovered that somewhere in the life of every one of those planes someone named Vygantas, or Vygantis, or in one case Vineman, made an appearance. Of course that could just be the stories being the stories, and since Gytis himself became something of a legend among fliers, it's possible that over the years he's become associated with them more as a matter of truth than of fact. He went on to become a senior engineer at Lockheed and was involved with the design of some of the most cutting edge airplanes in history. Turns out he had a knack, and then some. You'll forgive us for concluding his knack, and, perhaps, his family's was something more than that.

Kim's destiny and heroism lay on a different path. The folks who build today's modern stealth fighters and bombers would be quite jealous of her, because although she flies every week she only rarely appears as an errant blip on radar. Times being what they are, from time to time the Air Force will scramble fighters to intercept an unknown aircraft. The combat pilots who've been fortunate enough to be involved in one of those intercepts always end up flying in formation with her for a while, stunned that they are seeing an airplane they'd heard of only as a legend and a rumor. They never report what they've seen, which is one of the reasons you'll still hear stories about fighter pilots seeing UFOs. That's how they report those missions. There's an unspoken agreement among aviators to respect Kandy Kim. Without her they would lose one of the purest forms of magic left in the world.

Which brings us to our recommendation, and the end of this little volume of flying stories. In this day and age we've discovered magic can be difficult to come by. Everything has an explanation, and there are a lot of people who flat out refuse to believe in it.

If you find yourself losing the magic that makes life worth living, get in an airplane. Not a big jetliner but a little airplane, preferably with a single piston engine and no more than six seats. A plane where you can see not just out a little side window but 360 degrees around you. Maybe call an old friend who has her pilot's license, or go on a sightseeing flight from your local airfield. In a pinch, just post a note on the message board at the airport. Pilots are a generous lot and you'll find one who will give you a ride simply because he or she knows what you're looking for up there. Even if you're not quite sure.

Acknowledgments

The writer and the stories owe a debt of gratitude to Jeff Berg and Denny Luria, who believed from the start, to David Gonzalez who helped guide the ship, and to Tyson Cornell, Julia Callahan, Alice Marsh-Elmer, and everyone at Rare Bird Books who made it a reality. To Stephanie LeGras for a lifetime of love and support. To Susan R. Norton for inspiration that could never be replicated. To Max Ross, Robert "Rotten" Roman, Rachel Kondo, Darri Farr, and J. Ryan Stradal for editorial suggestions and endless encouragement. To Lou Mathews for mentorship. To those who are in this book in one way or another whether they know it or not: Dr. Neal Chawla, D. Brendan Holland, Danny Passman, Reveta Bowers, Tommy Zottner, Michael Vincent, David Cheng, Christopher "Chance" Rashad, Mary Lee Rybar, Manny Rodriguez, Emily Callaghan, David and Adam Iscove, Gytis Vygantis Sammy Sotoa, Nora Hall, Mary Cobb, Craig de Recat, Fernando Barragan, and Jason Alisharan. To my flight instructors and every pilot who taught me something about staying aloft and staying safe. Oh, and to Mark Hawes, if you're out there: *rice pudding.*